p n e u m a

a true fable

PATTI LYNNE

Dragonfly Productions
PO Box 25466
Tempe, AZ. 85285

Back Cover Images:
Photo of Gerti Mermelstein, Auschwitz Album, Public Domain courtesy of United States Holocaust Memorial Museum

Photo of Patti Lynne, courtesy of Patti Lynne

Design by *waynekehoe.com*

CONTENTS

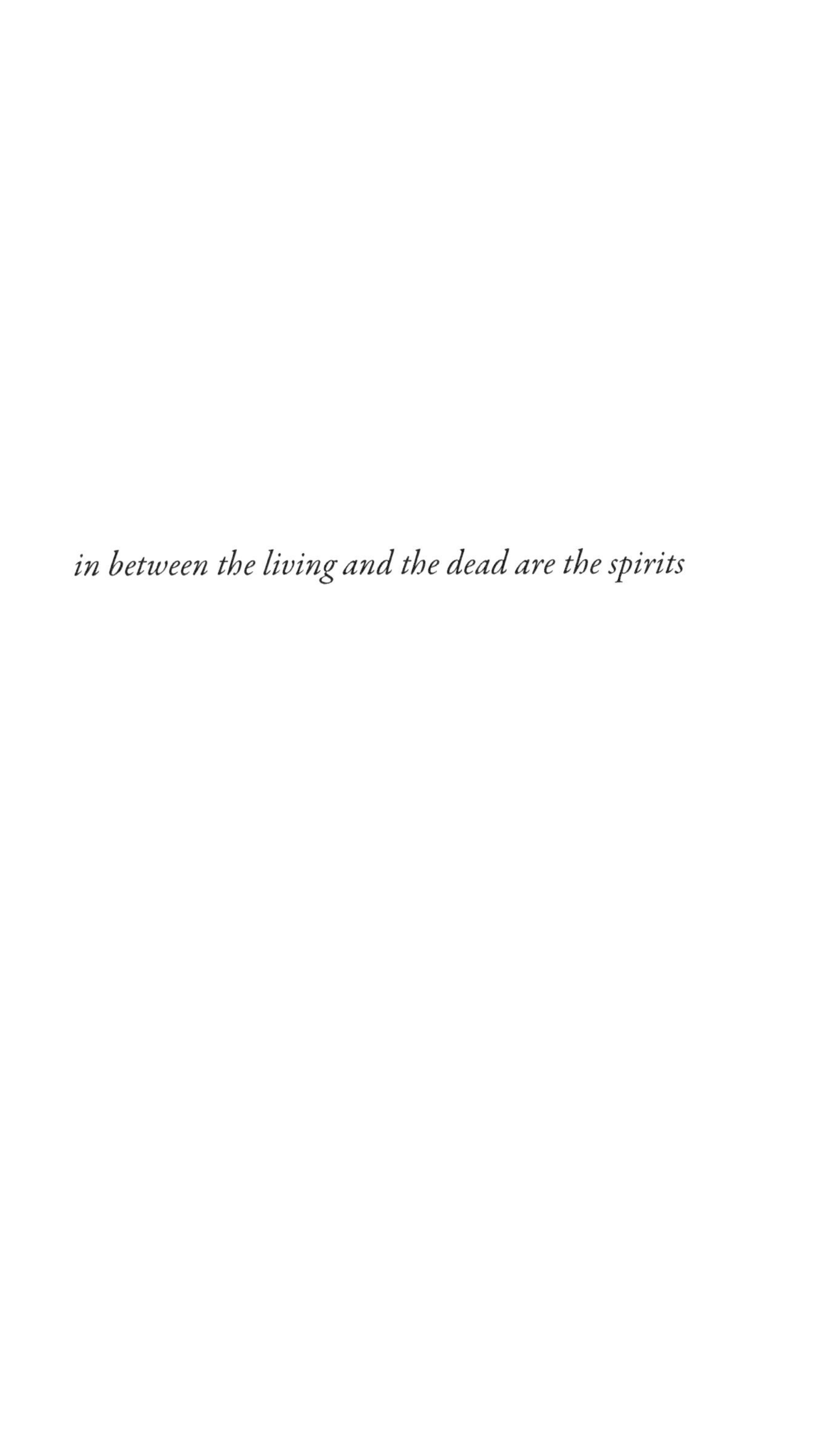
in between the living and the dead are the spirits

pneuma

pneuma

FOREWORD

I'm Patti, and mine is one of two intertwined stories in the pages that follow. My own transformational healing from childhood trauma to a miraculous re-birth unfolds exactly as it happened to me.

The other story took shape when a young spirit child literally appeared to me and guided me to Auschwitz-Birkenau on All Souls Day. Why would I fly all the way to Poland to be at the camp on November 2nd? Because I was invited.

Once present in the Birkenau grove, I understood why. It wasn't that hard to follow the steps laid out like breadcrumbs on a path. I did as I was told. What I didn't realize then, not fully, was that I wasn't just being asked to witness something. I was being asked to complete something. To speak for the unspeakable. To become a vessel for a tale that had waited decades to be told.

People often ask what I am doing in a story like this. I am not Jewish and I have no family connection to the Holocaust. But life—Spirit—has led me down a path I never could have imagined. My connection to the child who found me has revealed itself in visions, in dreams, in memories that didn't belong to me but somehow lived in me. It's a connection that defies logic and yet feels truer than anything I've ever known. It doesn't begin with me, and it doesn't end with me. It belongs to the thousands who were silenced. It belongs to all of us.

The story that follows isn't always easy. But it is deeply human. It is a story of unimaginable pain, yes—but also of profound healing, unexpected love, and the ways in which we carry one another, even across lifetimes.

I invite you to read with an open heart. You don't need to believe in spirit communication or everything that takes place herein. You only need to feel what's true for you.

May this story shine light on a place that has known such darkness. And may it remind us that healing—both personal and collective—is not only possible, but always waiting for us, just beneath the surface, when we are ready.

Patti Lynne

CHAPTER ONE

THEO CALLED THEM to the meeting in the sprawling oak tree, but they aren't gathering just yet. Some linger in the irregular angles of her branches. Others are relaxing on the tips of the thinnest of limbs, as light as the leaves themselves.

Theo, as always, is at the tree's highest point, signifying his powerful and unquestioned leadership. Dressed in a white, plain-fabric robe, he is tall with a long face surrounded by hair and beard. He senses the others' need to be absorbed by the tree and allows them all the time they want. Their presence causes a vibration throughout the old oak that resonates with each spirit attendee and penetrates to every distant root in the open field.

Late afternoon light slowly turns to dusk as the tree buzzes with dragonflies, ladybugs, bees, birds and fireflies creating color, sound, movement and light. As dusk fades, nothing but a twinkling shimmer remains.

As Theo calls the meeting to order with a lift of his hand, the spirits emerge throughout the tree to take part. His voice is warm and thoughtful, but absolute. "Welcome, all. On this day, I am setting into motion a Spirit Council mission of the highest order. While only a small group of you has been called into action, its importance is beyond measure. Simon has already been hard at work and, as our resident scholar, he shall now provide to us the mission's historical context."

Peering out shyly from his safe perch on a sturdy branch

connected to the main trunk of the tree, Simon slowly transforms to the man he was before he transitioned, in professorial clothing with dark-rimmed glasses, tousled thinning hair, and a quiet demeanor. It is evident that he enjoys time spent as his former self, no matter how brief, and communicates as a natural teacher. "The history of this mission began eighty years ago, in 1944. World War II was raging, the Nazis knew they were losing, and time was short. They became determined to rid one final country of its Jewish population. Hungary. Efforts were intensified to prepare Birkenau, also known as Auschwitz II, to handle more killings than had ever before been attempted at one location. Over fifty-six days, 434,000 Hungarian Jews were transported directly to the camp, as many as three transports daily with more than 3,000 people packed into cattle cars. 347,000 Hungarian Jews were gassed immediately upon arrival. 200,000 of them were children." Simon removes his glasses and bows his head out of respect for what he has just revealed. The other spirits begin a slow murmur as though they are unable to contain the knowing of that astounding statistic; and, with no place else to go, the energy escapes as a collective, mesmerizing sound.

"Grace will now explain what happened to the children, their mothers, grandparents, and the elderly once they arrived," Theo continued.

Grace is situated on a minor branch, comfortable on the breeze that occasionally makes it swing to and fro. She transforms from spirit to elderly, beloved grandmother wrapped in a white lace shawl covering the small floral pattern of her plain dress. She is delicate with pale, translucent skin that barely covers the bones beneath. Her eyes are as blue as the sea. She speaks slowly and haltingly, partly due to her age and partly due to the nature of her report.

"The journey from Hungary to the camp was arduous and many died along the way. Up to seventy people were crammed in each cattle car with no room to sit and no food or water for three days. Standing in human excrement with no knowledge of their destination or how long the journey would take, the airless, sweltering cattle car was shared by the living, the barely living, and the dead. Upon arrival, the survivors were unloaded and the women, children, and elderly were separated from the younger, stronger Jews capable of work. Those considered useless and chosen to die were marched across a field to a birch grove where they were told they would soon be given a shower and a hot meal. The Nazis wanted no panic or chaos in the peaceful beauty of the grove in stark contrast to the inevitable fate that awaited them a short walk down the path. Exhausted and full of false hope, some relaxed on the ground under the shade of the welcoming branches and some milled about, perhaps thinking it wouldn't take long for them to be escorted to where they would be staying. What they didn't know was these would be their last moments on earth."

Theo gives his spirits enough time to process Grace's remarks before speaking. "Our mission is to guard the souls of the children who lost their lives on the day they arrived at Birkenau. We will insure that upon their deaths, their spirits do not get trapped in the gas chamber or the camp, but instead, with our help, will find their way to the World to Come as quickly as possible. Because of the unique nature of this mission, we will be calling upon a human, known as Patti, to assist us." The spirits begin to buzz upon hearing the news of human involvement in a spirit mission. Theo quiets them and continues, "I know this is unusual, but you will see its importance as the mission unfolds. I will be very involved in preparing our human for her part when the time comes. And now may I present Batya, our mission leader. She will explain how you will assist in the creation of a soul sister to our human ally and the important role she will play."

Batya is flooded by a pale light source as she emerges from the tree. Her movement is graceful, elegant and effortless. She begins to transform into the young ballerina. Natural human talents, in her case, were simply enhanced when she unexpectedly became a spirit; and she makes a lovely dancer in white satin dress and toe shoes with her long hair in a bun. Her voice is as gentle and lilting as her movement. She describes the mission's first step, mimicking her words with movement. "I will take up residence in the grove, known as the 'little meadow of birches' translated from the German word Birkenau. I will be joined by a young spirit child. She will be embedded, as our seedling soul, with a poor Hungarian Jewish family and will be born to parents, a sister, and a loving grandmother who will not know, but will sense, that she is a special gift. They will name her Gerti. She will become a source of light and joy to the family and her village, but her real work begins when they are all transported to the camp. She is a part of me, a part of all of us. I will oversee her gradual development into a working spirit, and the two of us will manage the safe delivery of the souls of these children to the World to Come. Then she will invite her human soul sister, Patti, to the grove when it is her time." No questions are asked as to why a human will be needed in the grove after all the children's spirits have departed.

Batya extends her long arms to let the other spirits know it is time to prepare for the seedling transport. She captures a small beam of her own light and gathers it in her cupped hands until they begin to glow. The pale spirit light that always surrounds her expands to the group. They create a vibrant translucent circle of energy to act as a vessel that will deliver the seedling soul to the womb of the Hungarian Jewess who will become her mother. Batya releases the tiny package of light to the powerful spirit collective and with a dramatic flourish of rising energy, the seedling soul is on her way.

The soft light that emanates from the spirit gathering in the huge oak begins to dissolve. The meeting is adjourned.

CHAPTER TWO

In the only bedroom of a small, modest dwelling, a bare mattress lies on the floor. Mother is curled in pain as Grandmother wipes her forehead with a wet cloth. She also delivered her daughter's first child, Wally, in this same room. Wally, now nine-years old, is frozen at the bedroom's low doorway at not only the thought of her new sibling entering the world, but also everything that goes into it from the moment Mother's belly began to swell until now as she clutches Father's hand and asks him how a baby can possibly get from Mother's stomach to Grandmother's arms. He squeezes her hand with a smile and tells her to be patient and she will see.

Grandmother has now moved to the end of the mattress and is encouraging her daughter to push as hard as she can. Mother lets out a scream and pushes, but the baby does not appear. Suddenly, her body relaxes completely, her head turns to the side, and with what seems like no effort, the baby arrives as naturally as a child shooting down a slide head first. She is serene, pink and glowing, and, after a small gasp, begins breathing smoothly on her own. Then she looks around as if to welcome the family to her world rather than the other way around. She is named Gerti.

1953

The delivery room is chilly. The bed frame, the counter tops, and the cabinets are shiny metal. Mother is sedated and Doctor, in a mask and crisp white gown, works silently to deliver the baby under the starched sheet that lays over the stirrups. Because Mother is not awake, he doesn't announce the sex of the baby to anyone in the room. He does seem taken aback by a large birthmark on the child covering her right chest, arm, and back shoulder. He holds up the baby to examine it more closely and then hands it off to a nurse to finish with post-birth tasks. He snaps off his gloves, says he will speak to Mother about it when she awakens, and strides briskly out of the room.

In an equally cold recovery room, Doctor stands at Mother's bedside. He grasps the shiny bedrail rather than her hand to deliver the news that she has a healthy baby girl; and while the large port wine stain covering a significant part of the upper right side of her body looks alarming, it is probably just a cosmetic issue and he will refer her to a specialist. Later, Patti's grandmother, known to her family as Mammy, will declare that the stain was a result of lightning that shocked Mother at seven months pregnant while turning on a light during a thunderstorm in Mammy's living room in Sumter, South Carolina. Mother asks Doctor, "Did you say it is a girl?" because the nurse handed her the baby swaddled in a blanket and she hadn't yet looked at her gender or her purple mark. Doctor nods yes. She says "Oh dear, this isn't what we were expecting. He was to be our Thomas Daniel. We don't even have a girl's name picked out." As Doctor turns to walk away, he says, "Well, it is St. Patrick's Day, if that helps." So they choose the feminine of St. Patrick, name her Patricia, and call her Patti.

Mother won't know it for several months, but Patti will also develop two different colored eyes, one brown and one blue, along with her two different colored hands, arms and breasts. The specialist at Duke University says radiation is the only option to remove the stain but it will likely cause her arm to stop growing permanently. His advice is to take her home and love her the way she is.

Theo made his presence known at Patti's birth, in the earliest stages of preparing her to be his mission's human helper. With his ability to temporarily transfigure into a human, he inhabited Mother's military doctor to perfection. He wanted to make sure the child's disappointing gender and physical surprises did not negatively impact her introduction to the world. He was especially pleased with his gentle but successful suggestion of naming her after a saint. It would not be the first time Theo was there for her, not changing her already remarkable story, but making sure that story didn't change her remarkable spirit.

CHAPTER THREE

Behind Grandmother's full muslin skirt hides Gerti, now an animated little girl enjoying the game of pretending she can't be seen. Each time she peeks out to make sure Grandmother is paying attention—which she always is even when she pretends she's not—Gerti dissolves into giggles and wraps herself in the folds of the fabric again. Grandmother takes off her apron and ties it around and around little Gerti's tiny waist and then removes her kerchief and uses it to tie back Gerti's short, blonde hair. This leaves Grandmother's long hair loose down her back, creating a glimpse of her as a much younger woman. As Gerti spins around in her new outfit, she reaches in the apron pocket and finds a piece of candy. "A candy!" she screeches. "Is it for me? Please, please may I have it?" Grandmother says, "Yes, Gerti, but it is our secret" and puts her finger to her lips with a ssshhhhh. "I know," Gerti says in a fake whisper with a huge smile and slips the candy into her mouth. Grandmother claims back her apron and kerchief, lifts Gerti up to sit on the rough wood work counter, and begins to make the family's meager dinner. She peels and cuts potatoes and onions as Gerti places the pieces into the pot for tonight's soup. Grandmother dabs Gerti's eyes when the onions make them water.

Father arrives looking very tired, nearly hunched over from a long day's work. He makes his way slowly to a worn but comfortable chair and removes his hat, head drooping. Grandmother lifts Gerti down so she can go to him as she does every evening when he gets home. She approaches Father slowly, stops in front of his chair, places her hands lightly on his knees and asks permission with her eyes to come closer. He gives it. She crawls onto his lap and puts her tiny hands on his sad face. He softens, closes his eyes, and smiles while she snuggles into his chest.

Mother and Wally come through the door. Mother is gloomy, as usual, carrying a bag of potatoes. Wally has a loaf of crusty bread under her arm that she delivers to Grandmother with a hug. They hang their coats on hooks inside the door and Mother reaches into her pocket to show everyone a handful of yellow cloth stars. She grabs Gerti's coat off the hook, pins the yellow star onto the left chest, and gestures to Gerti to come put it on. She slips off Father's lap and eases into the tattered coat that Mother is holding for her, stepping away to model it like a fancy lady in the finest fur, twirling around to show it off. The family watches her antics with pure affection and amusement, but also a looming concern.

Grandmother tells the girls to take bowls and spoons to the table as she puts the bread on a board and delivers that herself. The girls play a hand game as they wait for dinner. Grandmother tells all to come to the table, ladles the soup into the bowls and passes them around. Father pulls bread hunks straight from the loaf with his bare hands, distributes them, then dips his into the lukewarm soup.

"From now on, whenever you go out you must make sure you have the yellow star on your jacket," says Mother, looking directly at the girls. Wally stops eating her soup, looking puzzled, and says, "But why, Mother? Why do we have to?" "You must. That is all," she responds. Wally persists, "But why? Why do we?"

Grandmother sees that Mother is getting cross and losing her patience. She says softly to the girls, "Because we are Jewish. So they can tell you are a Jew." She sees that the girls are confused and don't understand. "Finish your soup. It is time for bed."

Grandmother shepherds the girls into the bedroom where the bare mattress is still on the floor in exactly the same spot as the day each of the girls was born. A small pile of thin blankets is strewn on the floor nearby. Grandmother helps the girls take off their dresses but leaves their leggings and muslin slips on for sleeping. There isn't room for them to sleep on the mattress with Mother, Father and Grandmother, so she wraps them up tight together in a blanket, making a game of it, and they snuggle up to each other on the floor. Sleep comes quickly for Wally, but Gerti is feeling a sense of unease and lingers awake.

In the waning light, she can only see the shadows of her parents and grandmother as they quietly enter the bedroom. Mother and Father peel off their outer clothing, squat onto the thin mattress, lie down on their sides close together, he on the edge and she close behind him, not necessarily out of affection but because it is the only way there is room left for Grandmother to lie close to the edge of the other side. Grandmother checks on the girls, and Gerti pretends to be sleeping like Wally who has already drifted off. Gerti watches Grandmother slowly kneel down to roll onto the narrow edge of the bed that remains and try to cover herself with a blanket that is too small and thin to keep her warm. Gerti is overcome with emotion for this family that she has come to love while never losing sight of the reason she is there. She doesn't yet completely understand the reason, but senses that things are about to be put into motion. When everyone is asleep and breathing evenly, she slips out of her blanket roll and goes to the bare window. The moon is bright and shines a wide path through the room. She feels a chill and hugs herself tight. In the far distance, she sees a chimney with a brilliant flame escaping from the top. Not sure if she is awake or asleep, she asks God, "Is this a dream?"

CHAPTER FOUR

YOUNG PATTI WAS a world traveler by the time she was two- years-old, sailing to Europe on a big ship with her family. Mother was so seasick the whole time that she carried a brown paper bag containing an apple everywhere she went, the only thing she could keep down. The family settled in Holland, lived in a Dutch neighborhood, in a Dutch house. Because Patti and her sister shared a bedroom, they were given the use of the sunny third bedroom as a playroom and spent hours on the hardwood floor throwing tea parties, playing dolls, and painting their nails. The small garden in the back yard featured tulips.

From there it was on to Germany, but this time home was a large apartment building shared with other American military families. Across the street was a beautiful forest that was fun to explore. When they went deep enough into the trees, there were small carnivals with giant box swings that you could coax over the top of the bar if you were brave enough.

Next stop was a small radar site in Northern California. Remote by necessity, the Air Force built twenty-seven small homes for the families. There wasn't much to do, so Kathy taught her little sister to read prior to starting kindergarten. They formed a singing duo and performed in base talent shows but mostly the living room. Patti started first grade in a class that was four rows of first graders and two rows of second graders. After just a few months, her teacher asked Mother and Father if she could move her to the two rows of second graders so she could be more challenged. It was agreed and, at the end of the year, Mrs. Scarmella wrote in her own hand on Patti's report card that this student was promoted to Grade Three. It was the first time she skipped a grade.

Patti found it difficult to navigate the challenges that came with her large red—but sometimes purple when she was cold—birthmark. She was tired of the other kids staring at her and making fun. She formulated a plan to personally ask God to remove it right away.

Ready to put the plan into action, Patti pulled on her long flannel nightgown and smiled as Mother tucked her in and turned off the overhead light as she left. The moon played her part by shining through the window over her bed like a theatrical spotlight, creating a wide path of brightness that Patti considered a personal invitation from God on high to discuss her situation. She climbed out of bed, got down on her knees bathed in the moonlight with hands folded, and spoke out loud: "Dear God, every Sunday morning I put on my dress and petticoat, white socks, patent leather shoes and lace gloves. So I guess you could say I am a pretty good Catholic, or at least a well-dressed one. I say my prayers before bed every single night. Between you and me, I don't know the difference between asking you for a favor and praying for something—is there one? Because I want to do this right. I need a good outcome. So here's the thing. I was born with a big birthmark, but you already know that. They call it a port wine stain. I'm just a little girl and I don't really like thinking of myself as stained. And everyone stares at me which I don't mind if I am singing and dancing or something like that. But this isn't the good kind of staring. This is a lot of whispering and pointing—and kids can be cruel, you know. And don't even get me started about the bathing suit problem. So here's my plan. Tonight, I am going to stay up all night long and never fall asleep, not one time. I will pray to you, God, over and over, to remove this birthmark before morning. Please." She made the sign of the cross with her right hand, forehead to chest to left shoulder and then right, and looked up at the ceiling as if to make sure He was paying attention. She crawled back under the covers, laid on her back, pulled her arms out and clasped her hands over her chest, eyes wide open. "I won't go to sleep all night long. I will keep praying. Dear God, please take away my birthmark by morning, please take away my birthmark by morning, please take away my ...." Despite her best efforts to keep going, her head fell over to one side as she began to nod off.

Theo stayed with Patti throughout the night. He knew this was the first of many monologues that she would create to understand her own life. She didn't need his help, as this special skill came naturally to her; but she thrived on his presence.

As the sun began to rise, Patti rubbed her eyes and suddenly remembered that she put her plan into place the night before, failing to admit that she had fallen asleep. She ripped off the covers and pulled up the long right sleeve of her nightie to see her arm. "It's still there!" angrily addressing God directly. "Why didn't you take it away? I prayed so hard! And never fell asleep, not once. I'm mad at you!" She began to cry, then sob into her pillow, because she knew that her birthmark *was* actually God's plan. She just didn't like it.

pneuma

pneuma

CHAPTER FIVE

Batya gives her fledgling spirit as much time as possible to enjoy being a little girl in a loving family. But she knows it is almost time for Gerti to take on the role for which she has been created. She also knows it begins in earnest this very day.

It starts just as any other. Grandmother stands in the doorway behind Gerti, coat in hand, encouraging her to go out into the cobblestone street and play in the early spring sunshine with the neighborhood boys. They are much older, almost teenagers, but they have a sweet spot for the spirit child. Their teasing is joyful, never mean, always protective, and they enjoy having her join in their games and small adventures. Today it is to use a stick to hit a beanbag: hastily assorted pebbles, and small rocks in a piece of burlap tied up with a string. She is feeling shy and hesitates as Grandmother assures her it will be fun. The boys are rambunctious because it has been raining for days and they are happy to be outdoors. They spot Gerti and call out to her, "Hey Gerti! Come play with us!" She shyly wanders over, looking back at Grandmother in the doorway for encouragement.

Janos, a gangly boy, gently pulls her in and hands her the stick. He mimics how she should hold it with both hands to get ready for the throw and helps her get in position. Laszlo, a much stockier young teenager, holds up the beanbag to show her and inches closer than where he stands to pitch it to the boys and yells out, "When you see it coming, hit it as hard as you can!" tossing it gently towards her. She swings the stick, misses the ball by a mile, and twirls around giggling, "Again...again!" which prompts laughter from her playmates.

Sandor, the zany one in the group, approaches her to assist saying, "Here, Gerti girl, watch me!" He takes the stick from her, showing off, and steps up to receive the throw and swings wildly. The unexpected whiff twirls him all the way around and he throws his head back to enjoy the feeling of being out of control, laughing, and then losing his balance. He begins to stagger and fall backwards, almost in what appears to be slow motion, hitting the back of his head hard on the cobblestone. He is knocked out cold, motionless on the street. Janos and Laszlo are terrified, frozen in fear.

Gerti rushes to Sandor's side, kneels beside him and lays her head on his chest, extending her small arms across him in a sacred embrace. She feels herself fully as a spirit for the first time and radiates a white light that surrounds her and Sandor's body. Batya appears, taking shape at Gerti's side. She has never shown herself fully to the child, but Gerti knows she is her guide. Batya, in her gentlest voice filled with concern, says quietly, "I know you want to save him, Gerti. But it is better to let Sandor go now and you can help him find his way to the World to Come." Gerti is upset because she knows instinctively that she can bring Sandor back to life, asking "But why *can't* I save him?" Batya speaks patiently, but firmly, "I know it is hard to understand why letting him go is better than saving his life. But there are things that you cannot yet know." Gerti begins to soften because she knows Batya has much more experience in these matters and naturally trusts her. She also knows every spirit has a purpose and that she is too new to even know what her purpose is. Nevertheless, she is still a child seeing death for the first time, knowing she can stop it, and not being allowed to use that power. She becomes quiet and pensive, trying to accept what she is being told. Batya responds, "You are feeling something familiar about attending to him at his time of close death. But that familiarity comes not from the past. It is borne of the future. You cannot understand that now. But you will. Soon enough.

Gerti cradles Sandor, bringing him even closer into the halo of her spirit light. She closes her eyes as if to create a kind of space and permission for him to go as a shadow rises from his body and ascends. Gerti stands to see him off, slightly amazed at what she has just done. Batya places her arm around Gerti as they look up.

Janos and Laszlo begin to stir, confused about what has just happened. Staying close together, they slowly approach Sandor's motionless body. It's their first time witnessing death also.

CHAPTER SIX

PATTI FELT LONELY and small in the big corner bedroom of the family's third floor apartment in Ankara, Turkey. She and Kathy had always shared a room as close sisters who often only had each other after so many moves and foreign addresses. The two girls initially moved in to the big sunny bedroom with the French doors that led out to a narrow balcony where they could see the roof of the Russian Embassy at the end of the narrow downhill street. The only time they ever saw activity on that roof was the day that President Kennedy was assassinated. With no radio or television to rely on, they heard the news from the Turkish landlady who knocked on the door, put her index finger to her temple and said "Boom, boom... President Kennedy!" On that day, there was a lot of celebrating on the roof.

For some reason, Father decided that Kathy should be moved to the small middle bedroom with the tiny window even though she didn't ask for her own room. Now when Father came in at night to lay with Patti, and threw his arm over her stomach, she had no one to distract him on her behalf, which Kathy often did, or talk to about it when he finally got tired and left for his own room. Things were never quite the same with her sister after the move. She was never quite the same.

Theo knew that Patti was becoming more anxious in her family life and often had a bad stomach ache, diagnosed as "nervous stomach." He also knew that she carried the family secrets in herself, even though she didn't consciously know what they were yet. The only way to deal with that stress was for her body to respond in some physical way that she could describe as an ailment. But he saw her taking on more and knew she must learn that she could not become a receptacle for everyone's pain or her stomach ache could turn into something much worse.

Theo rarely intervened in Patti's life, but on this night, he became Father for a distinct purpose. He came in to check on her, saying that he had noticed she seemed upset, and sat next to her on the bed to talk. He sees that she is trembling and asks, "What's wrong?" She whispers, "I can't feel my legs. I think they're paralyzed." "You walked into your room a little while ago and climbed into bed," Theo answers. "Has anything changed since then?" In a very small voice, she answers, "I don't know." Giving her a moment, he continues, "Did something happen at school today? Something upsetting?" Theo has the benefit of knowing the answers before he asks the questions, but he gently guides her through each step of realization. "I think so." Theo asks her to tell. "There is a new boy at my school. He has to use these heavy metal crutches around his arms to drag his legs behind him. He was working so hard just to make it to his classroom on time. I felt so sorry for him. . . and for his struggle." Theo tries to put the pieces together for her. "That may be why you are having trouble feeling your own legs. I think you feel so deeply for his suffering that you have taken it on yourself. Do you think that is possible?" "I guess so. I didn't mean to," she says.

"It is a very good quality of yours to care that much about another student. But it would be best if you did not take on his illness and pain in your own body. You know that you can't really take someone else's pain away by taking it for yourself. It is good to care. And you are a good person, Patti. But you must learn to separate the pain of others from your own. His legs are paralyzed, not yours." He pulls up her covers and tucks her in tight. "There, do you think the feeling might be coming back?" "Maybe a little," Patti pauses, "but I feel kind of...guilty." "Because you can walk and he can't?" Theo asks. "Yes," Patti says. "It seems so unfair." Theo continues, "Patti, that is his story, not yours. You may help him in ways that only you can. But not by hurting yourself. Do you understand?" "I think so," Patti says quietly, then reaches out for Theo's hand. "Will you stay with me?" "Yes," says Theo. "Until you fall asleep."

CHAPTER SEVEN

THE VILLAGE IS FILLED with people who have gathered to lay Sandor to rest on this early spring afternoon. The wooden box is being carried through the narrow street with his mother and other family walking behind. A rabbi leads the procession, reading scripture along the way. "You who dwells in the shelter of the Most High, who abides in the shadow of the Omnipotent, I say of the Lord who is my refuge and my stronghold, my God in who I trust, that He will save you from the ensnaring trap, from the destructive pestilence."

The group approaches the grave site that has been prepared under a beautiful old tree and lowers the small box in the ground. A chair has been placed for Sandor's mother beside the grave as she is overwrought.

The rabbi continues, "He will cover you with His pinions and you will find refuge under His wings; His truth is a shield and an armor."

Janos approaches and throws dirt on to the box, then steps back.

"You will not fear the terror of the night, nor the arrow that flies by day, the pestilence that prowls in the darkness, nor the destruction that ravages at noon." The rabbi grows more intense with each word.

Laszlo steps up next, throws a handful of dirt on top, and returns to Janos's side. It has been hard for them to understand the death of their friend. They had been inseparable ever since.

"A thousand may fall, at your left side, and ten thousand at your right, but it shall not reach you. You need only look with your eyes, and you will see the retribution of the wicked."

Sandor's mother stands and walks slowly towards the opening in the ground and throws a handful of dirt on the wooden box that holds her son's body, eyes cast down with a fixed gaze.

"Because the Lord is my shelter and you have made the Most High your haven, no evil will befall you, no plague will come near your tent. For He will instruct His angels in your behalf, to guard you in all your ways."

Sandor's mother is frozen in place, overcome with grief. Gerti steps up, gently takes her hand and leads her back to the chair, helping her sit. She leans over and whispers in his mother's ear, at which time her white spirit light envelops them both. With Gerti's arms lovingly encircling her neck, the boy's mother closes her eyes, deeply comforted by the words of the small spirit.

CHAPTER EIGHT

On a late spring morning so early it is still dark, men bang on the door and tell Gerti's family to get up, get dressed, collect a few things, and get outside. They do as they are told and quickly realize that all the Jewish families are being rousted and herded into the street in the same way. Gerti and Wally cling to each other while Grandmother, Mother, and Father quickly grab some things to take.

They are held for two weeks in an abandoned brick factory with walls that are literally crumbling or have already fallen. Without a roof, when it gets windy and rainy, the family shivers and clings to each other all night long. There is very little food or water, no blankets, and no bathroom facilities.

One day they are moved to a train station where it seems likely they will be loaded onto the train, but it doesn't look like it's meant for people. The cars are big, empty boxes lined up as far as the eye can see down the track. After a long wait, the big sliding door to each car is pushed open where one small window provides almost no light. Everyone is pushed forward and thrown into a car. There are too many in each car to sit down, or barely even breathe. The family manages to stay close together. After a long wait, the train starts to move, very slowly.

Countless hours pass. Gerti and Wally try to squat in the corner, but it is hard when everyone is crushing against them. There is no place to go to the bathroom so everyone tries to hold it, but can't;

so the smell makes the air thick and putrid. Some people panic and start screaming and fainting, mostly women. The others do their best to watch over the children who are tired and scared and upset. No one knows how long it has been, but it seems like many days. It is hard to tell if it is day or night and the hours just go on and on.

Gerti begins to feel as if there must be something she can do to assist with the absolute misery on this train. She is now a working spirit, not a four-year-old child traveling with her family from Hungary to somewhere probably worse than where they have already been. It is as if she is waking up to the calling that has sent her there in the first place.

An old man and his wife cling to each other. They are having trouble standing after so many hours in the stifling box car. The woman is buckling and struggling to breathe, while her husband tries to support her weight. He isn't succeeding but won't let her go. Gerti attends to the wife who desperately tries to stay with her husband but cannot find the will. She gasps, stops breathing, and her body goes limp. He begins to realize that she has passed and quietly wails in excruciating pain. The realization has taken the life and breath out of him and they crumple to their demise, still holding hands. Gerti makes sure they stay connected, both in the train and as they prepare to find their way to the World to Come. Often, souls wish to stay in the earthly plane for a while longer to get their spiritual affairs in order before they depart. But in this case, their only spiritual affairs were each other, so the two souls ascend immediately with utter grace and beauty out of a place of such deep human suffering. As Gerti witnesses their departure, she senses what lies ahead.

Wally reaches out and folds her little sister into her own body, just as she has always done at night when Grandmother rolled them up together in the blanket. But this time it isn't to stay warm: it is to stay alive. Gerti thinks to herself, "I know she needs me to take care of her. But, because she is older, I will do that by making her feel she is taking care of me."

The train slows, finally stops, and the door to the box car is thrown open to the blinding light of day. Soldiers scream at those who have survived the journey to get off the train. The men try to assist the elderly and the mothers with the big step down. Once on the ground, a selection takes place. The stronger, younger men along with older boys and fit women without children are grouped together. Mothers and their children along with the elderly and sick are moved to their own line. There is a sense of panic about this family separation. Gerti waves to Father from her line, but he doesn't see her because she is so small and there are so many people. She loses sight of him as his group is marched away.

Mother, Grandmother, Wally, and Gerti are led with the other mothers, grandparents, and children across a big open field. They trudge slowly because so many are old and already exhausted, hungry, and thirsty. The mothers are carrying young children in their arms and holding the hands of those old enough to walk on their own. They are led to a grove of beautiful birch trees across a soft path from a lake filled with the ashes of those that came before them. There are hundreds of people in the grove and they are told to wait there for a hot meal. Mother, Grandmother, and Wally sit on the ground surrounded by the few small items they had been allowed to bring. For the moment, they feel relief from the horror of the train ride and hope that they will be safe in this new home.

CHAPTER NINE

PATTI WAS FOUR-YEARS-OLD when she was chosen to play a baby in a fancy carriage for a stroll across the stage during a dance recital put on by the Americans stationed in Ramstein, Germany in the mid-1950's. Frank Sinatra sang "Love and Marriage" while Patti was pushed in the carriage wearing a beautiful white ruffled dress and matching bonnet carrying a big lollypop. She also danced with her class in a red satin tutu with white fur around the neckline and ballet shoes with satin ribbons crossed around her ankles.

When Patti was eight-years-old, she was in fifth grade, having skipped another school year. Mother was cast in *The Drunkard*, a melodrama, as a dancer wearing a full blue and white checkered skirt and a frilly white petticoat underneath. When rehearsals began, the director was frustrated in his search for a young girl to play the drunkard's daughter. He confided in Mother that he had been forced to cast a young girl who was not right for the part because she did not fit the physical type of a child who was nearly starving after having been abandoned by her father, the drunkard. Mother told him she knew a young actress who was very slight and played younger than she was, also a talented and experienced performer. He was very interested and Mother brought Patti in for a secret audition. The director cast her on the spot and then had the unpleasant job of breaking the news to his original ten-year-old choice that she would not be playing the role. Patti was thrilled to get the part, but felt very bad for her friend and across the street neighbor— who was disappointed but so kind that she was actually happy for Patti. The awkward situation didn't stop the girls from playing together after school, dancing to "The Monster Mash" at Halloween and learning every word of Lesley Gore's "It's My Party" so they could sing it together over and over.

As a young junior high student in the brand-new American school in Turkey, Patti caught the eye of her French teacher, Mr. Parker, who was directing the spring play, *The Miracle Worker*. He approached her in the hall one day, led her to an empty classroom, and asked her to pick up a chair and throw it as far across the room as possible. He was impressed with her strength and offered her the role of Helen Keller. It would be a big commitment, he told her, as they would rehearse for months. She and her parents enthusiastically agreed. It was Patti's first attempt at dramatic material that wasn't centered around song and dance. Mr. Parker rehearsed her blindfolded for the first few months to help her experience the handicap of blindness. She bonded with the older high school student who played Helen's teacher, Annie Sullivan, and relied on her as a guide throughout the grueling experience of rehearsals and performances. By this time, acting wasn't a hobby, it was a calling.

Upon the family's return to the States, Patti was lucky enough to attend one high school for the entire four years, the longest her family had ever stayed in one place. She continued to perform and train as a dancer. Her drama teacher, Mrs. Bedinger, asked if she planned to major in theatre in college. Patti didn't even know there was such a major, but with strong encouragement from her teacher, announced to Mother and Father that she would be looking for a good theatre department for college. Father did not agree, but eventually gave in.

Patti had an accomplished acting career first at a small private liberal arts school and then for the next three years at a major university. She had many significant roles both in musicals and dramas, but it was one in particular that reached her in a different way. It was a part in a summer show, not nearly as important as her recent role in Shakespeare's *Henry V* playing Princess Catherine, a role she performed entirely in French. The show was *Archy and Mehitabel*, in which Patti was cast as a ladybug who was very sassy and bright. She communicated by jumping on the keys of a typewriter keyboard painted on a trampoline tilted toward the audience. This required a unique skill set and a certain physical fearlessness, but Patti took the ladybug character very seriously. In the same show, she also played a lightning bug, hiding a somewhat clunky battery pack in her costume so she could light up while dancing.

She went to visit the director before rehearsal one day and found him in his office. With her usual energy, she burst in excitedly. He responded, "Ever hear of knocking?" Patti sat in the chair across from his desk and said "Sorry, don't mean to bother you, but I have a few notes I would like to discuss about my character." The director shrugged and said "Patti, your character is a ladybug. I'm not sure we need to spend too much time on this. She's sassy and writes notes by jumping on a trampoline that looks like typewriter keys and sings every now and then." Patti grew anxious because she was trying to have a serious conversation. "Yes, but I feel a close connection to this ladybug, like I'm a part of her or maybe becoming her, and I think there is more to her than that. Did you know in England they call them ladybirds? And some like to call them ladybird beetles or lady beetles as they aren't really bugs, you know. But I'm good with ladybug so I'm not asking for a character name change or anything." The director looked out at her over his reading glasses, mildly amused, "Good to know."

Patti's demeanor was starting to change now. Theo was close by but didn't intervene, just observed. She became increasingly passionate, "I have also learned that ladybugs symbolize protection, healing and grace. They are considered spiritual and can protect flowers and plants from pests and bugs. And they symbolize metamorphosis because they have many life-stages, like dying and being reborn." The director leaned in to her, "I think it's great that you are so engaged with your character, Patti. It is unusual for an actress to play a ladybug and by golly, you are making the most of it, but this isn't Shakespeare. And I have a lot of work to do." He looked down at the stack of papers on his desk to signal to her that it was time for her to leave. Patti missed the message, and continued. "But why does a ladybug poet mean less than a Shakespearian heroine?" Becoming increasingly irritated, the director said, "Because one was created by Don Marquis, that great American New York newspaper humorist and the other by William Shakespeare. Remember him? You recently played Princess Catherine in *Henry V*!" Patti continued, "You know how much Shakespeare means to me. But while one play may be more eloquently stated, does that make its story any more or less meaningful than the other? Where would we be if only writers as gifted as Shakespeare had the right to tell stories?" "I see your point, Patti. But what we are working with now is a ladybug. I will go with poet if you insist. But let's not overthink it."

Patti, barely listening now as she seemed in her own world, stood slowly from her chair, dramatically continuing the story as a monologue. She seemed almost disassociated, transported as though the story was being channeled through her, not told by her. Theo understood this progression, moved a little closer and held her space as she continued. "During the reign of King Robert II of France, a man is sentenced to death by guillotine, all the while proclaiming his innocence. With his head on the guillotine, a ladybug lands on his neck, distracting and upsetting the executioner. He tries to shoo the ladybug away, but she returns each time. Now King Robert is a man of devotion and he declares the little beetle the *bête à bon Dieu*, the creature of Good God. He insists on halting the execution and frees the man, who is later found to be innocent." Patti was gradually returning to the moment and leaned across the director's desk for emphasis, "I really, really feel the power of this little creature and I must honor her with my performance!" She was in tears now, head bowed, overcome with emotion. Theo was proud of the connection she had made and collected her in his presence.

The director was both puzzled and impressed with what he had witnessed and said awkwardly, "I understand, Patti. That's good work. See you in rehearsal." But he wasn't being truthful. He didn't understand. Not at all.

CHAPTER TEN

For the time being, things are calm in the birch grove where hundreds of Hungarian Jews are waiting for something. They don't know what, but can it really be worse than two miserable weeks in the burned-out brick factory ghetto followed by the three day train journey, the horrors of which were beyond the imagination of any one of them? No, they collectively choose to believe it could not be worse.

Wally, Grandmother, and Mother are seated under the grove's Mother Tree, resting. Gerti is standing close by, sensing the spirit work to be done. As Gerti's spirit light begins to surround her, the rest of the grove dims and seems to freeze in time. She moves toward Laszlo and Janos who are sitting close together, pretending to one another that they aren't as scared and confused as they are. Gerti appears before them, bright in her light, nearly translucent, and coaxes them up to start a game of tag. They begin to regain their energy and start to chase each other, with a reckless abandon that reflects their pent-up emotional panic. They play in their own light, disconnected from the others in the grove, having fun, reconnecting to the affection they have always felt in their lifelong shared experiences. But at this moment, those memories are instantly bolder and clearer and fill them with joy and profound friendship. The boys fall to the ground laughing and wrestling.

Gerti moves on to a tiny young girl, shy, sitting next to her mother, trying to hide behind her skirt. Gerti smiles warmly and gently extends her hand. Now fully in Gerti's spirit light, the child takes her hand and stands. Gerti holds out her other hand and the child grasps it as Gerti begins to playfully spin them in circles. The tiny child smiles and drops her head back to feel the motion. They come to a stop and the child takes a moment to regain her balance. Gerti leans down to her and points to a very old gentleman sitting alone on the ground, suggesting that she approach him to say hello, knowing how much a little kindness would mean to him. Emboldened by Gerti's guidance, the tiny child slowly approaches the old man. She smiles at him. He doesn't respond. She gently sits down next to him and leans in. He is stiff at first, but then turns his face toward the tiny child and allows himself a slight smile, letting her soothe his misery. She puts her head on his shoulder and loops her arm through his. He is overwhelmed by her simple gesture of kindness.

Gerti returns to Wally, who is looking lost, and picks up a ladybug, letting it explore from hand to hand, turning one over the other to keep the creature close. She leans down to show Wally, who giggles with delight. Gerti coaxes the ladybug into her hands and they begin to glow.

A German soldier with a camera briskly enters the grove with hat pulled down low and lines up in front of the small crowd gathered under the Mother Tree. Gerti understands what he is doing at this moment, but the others don't, although some are looking his way with curiosity. Gerti extends her shining hands to him, now closed tight around the ladybug, and smiles, naturally lighting his upcoming photograph. He snaps the shudder and, in that instant, captures the last moments of their earthly, ordinary lives in what would live to be an extraordinary, historical document.

CHAPTER ELEVEN

PATTI AND MOTHER were living in a small townhouse while Father was in Southeast Asia, stationed in Thailand and flying missions over North Vietnam. Patti had been accepted into the theatre department of the nearby university she had chosen and, it having been determined she was still too young to go away to school, Mother had come to live with her. Kathy was away from home attending school. She decided she would marry a young man she met when he knocked on the door selling curb address painting services. A charming Southerner with a sweet drawl, he would inherit the family dry-cleaning business and take Kathy to live in the deep South. But the wedding would take place over Thanksgiving weekend where Patti and Mother were living. Father was taking a short leave from his base in Thailand to attend.

Mother chirped on about how they had been separated for six months and how excited she was for their sexual reunion. It wasn't unusual for her to share such things with Patti, who was completely inexperienced as to the sex but very experienced with such conversations.

A party was planned for the night before the wedding. There was drinking and celebrating and Father chose this time to deliver Patti's gift, a tradition whenever he traveled home from another country. It was Barbra Streisand's *A Christmas Album* in the form of an eight-track tape. A huge fan, Patti was thrilled and couldn't wait to hear it, rushing off to the older model Cadillac parked in the carport which was the only eight-track player available.

Happy to escape the chaos of the party and hide in the dark car, she was deeply enjoying her private holiday moments with Barbra. Father appeared out of the dark and slid into the passenger seat. Smelling of alcohol, Patti felt that familiar feeling like when he would come into her room and lie close to her, a freezing in her body, a fear of moving. It always seemed best to be as still as possible until it passed. This time it was different. With Barbra's Christmas music swelling, Father began to make out with Patti, just as any clumsy young boy would do at the drive-in on a date. He leaned in to kiss her sloppily and his hands began to roam across her chest, lingering on her right breast, but continually moving, almost in a rhythm. This molestation seemed oddly familiar, even though he had never touched her in this way before. He seemed so comfortable with his technique, his approach, as though he had done it many times before. Confused and shocked, Patti reached for the door handle and fumbled her way out of the car. She told no one. Because even she didn't know what had just happened to her.

Kathy married the next day. She seemed dazed and uncertain as to what she was doing, almost like watching herself participate. For the first time, Patti knew how that felt. Her sister waved goodbye as they left for their honeymoon, but it looked more like a desperate escape.

Over that one weekend, Father had his sexual reunion with Mother, sat in the locked bathroom with Kathy as she took her pre-wedding bath, introduced Patti to his sexual favors in the car, all the while looking forward to returning to his live-in lover in Thailand.

Theo stayed close to Patti as she slowly began to become aware of the paternal sexual abuse she had sensed most of her life, and experienced firsthand the night before Kathy's wedding as Father made the gruesome transition from one daughter to the next. Theo understood that Patti would be the only survivor of the four members of her family even though she would fight for many years to save them all. Finally saving herself would be the most necessary and important spiritual work of her life.

CHAPTER TWELVE

A GUARD APPEARS in the eerie stillness of the birch grove where those who are waiting continue to do so. He has a baton and uses it to prod people to get up and get moving. It takes them a while due to their physical fatigue and fear. He grows impatient, louder, and more aggressive. Gerti flits about like the ladybug who is now attached to her coat collar, watching over her flock, knowing these moments are precious. She smiles at the tiny girl to make sure she understands to take the old man's hand, help him up, and walk him out of the grove. He moves slowly and the tiny girl patiently moves at his pace, shielding him from the roaming guard. Laszlo and Jonas are still laughing and shoving each other playfully down the path. Gerti takes Wally's hand, then helps Grandmother up with the other hand, and walks them out of the grove with Mother following. Gerti extends her spirit light to all those who are headed down the path until they are one under her protection, offering the healing and grace they will need in advance. It is too late for their human bodies, but not for their souls.

The grey concrete floors, walls, and ceiling of the chamber greet their naked bodies with the cold foreshadowing of what is immediately to come. Quickly becoming terrified, they reach for one another, gasping for air, pushing toward the exit. The struggle turns to quiet.

Gerti leaves her temporary human body and facilitates the escape of the dead. The cement boundaries of the chamber offer no resistance to the congregation of souls beginning the various stages of their journey to the World to Come. At once they all form a translucent mass; but as she wanders the space, they begin to sort themselves out, beginning the process of moving towards resolution which, under the circumstances, does not come naturally. The younger travel easily. The elderly are more resolved, trying to make sense of this terrible end to their long, exhausting lives, having at least expected, or hoped for, respect for their advanced years in passing. Gerti understands that this mass transition requires some type of procedure to accommodate the process so they may move on as soon as possible and not get trapped in this place.

She looks to Batya and Theo, both watching over Gerti's work from the Mother Tree, and asks for help. They join her and begin gathering the spirits for final transition. Gerti positions herself on the path to the light where she can assist each one in their final preparation. First they will express and process whatever is needed to bring their human life experience to a close, after which she will escort them to the brilliant passage out. Batya and Theo begin by working with the children.

Wally appears and begins the reflective process, "I am nothing. Once the only child of my parents and only grandchild of my mother's mother. My parents thought they could never have another child. We were all so happy and surprised when we realized there was a brother or sister on the way, but my mother couldn't imagine how it could be possible. And then the child was born. She was different, our Gerti. In a way, she healed us from our small, simple lives. Like a beam of light. I thought nothing bad would happen to us because we had Gerti." She smiles at the thought as Gerti beams affection to her human sister. "And yet here we are. Dead!" She says this as though astonished but with no anger, moving suddenly to resolve. "I guess some things are more powerful than light." Gerti allows Wally to see her and be with her, reaching out her small hand to lead her along the pathway.

Janos and Laszlo appear next, deeply connected spirits, nearly one. Janos takes in the new form of his spirit brother, beginning to realize what has happened to them. "We're just kids. Grew up together. Spent every day together. Like brothers." Laszlo continues, "We don't even know where we are. A long train ride took us away from home. It was tough, but we knew we could get through anything together. Always have." Their arms are still entwined as Janos continues, "They sent us to that grove and said we should wait for a meal and to see where we were going to stay. And we were just hoping we would be together. We got bored so we were running around and playing just like we do at home. Just like always." The boys laugh at how they still speak the same, even now. Laszlo says, "We thought this was a shower." Janos adds, "But it's not. Our mothers and grandmothers and little sisters and brothers came in here, too. We weren't even near them because we didn't know it was the last time we would be together." He tightens at the thought of this overwhelming guilt and grief. And Laszlo, conjuring the pain leading up to their demise, observes, "And then it seemed like we couldn't breathe…. and it hurt to breathe. Everyone started to panic and tried to climb over the others to get some extra air. The little ones were nearly crushed at the bottom of the pile. I saw my mother and my baby brother turn blue and stop moving as other people piled up on top of them." Janos finishes the thought, "And we couldn't do anything. We held on to each other until we passed out." They pull closer to one another and Laszlo says pensively, "We sure didn't know this was coming. This isn't what we thought life was going to be like." Janos finishes the thought, "And now we have no idea what is next." They move slowly to acceptance. Gerti shows herself to them and they reach out with delight, "Hey, look. It's Gerti girl!" She begins to run down the pathway knowing they will playfully follow her.

The tiny girl, still holding the hand of her newest and last friend, arrives next on the path. The old man begins his reflection and seems to be processing for the two of them due to her tender age. "I was an old man, alone in this world, poor and miserable. After my wife died, I was so lonely…. so angry. I could not find happiness or faith. My village did what they could for me when they could. I was rounded up with the others, sent to the ghetto, and put on the train. I did not think it was possible for me to survive that journey. When we arrived, I was shoved into a line and marched to the grove of birch trees where I sat by myself, exhausted and broken." He softens as he turns his gaze to the tiny girl. "And then this tiny child approached me, smiled and without even asking, sat down next to me. I didn't say she couldn't." He had a twinkle in his eye at the thought of that moment. "I didn't want her or anyone to know, but it felt good to have her next to me. A child who wasn't afraid of my hard face and old body. She made me feel loved in such a short time. That was the last thing that happened to me before ending up here. She was so young, I am sure her kindness to me was her very first mitzvah. The main reward for her solo mitzvah was reserved for the World to Come. We did not know that reward would come within the hour. I hope I get to see my wife again. I would like her to meet my tiny friend." He beams down at the child, ready to move forward. Gerti escorts them down the path and to the light.

Sandor's mother appears for processing. "It was three weeks ago today that I lost my only child, Sandor, while he was playing in the street with the other boys. I thought it was the worst thing that could happen to a woman, losing a child. But this. I don't know what is going on here but it seems something unimaginable, something God could not intend. How could I know that gratitude would be an emotion that could possibly be felt where my Sandor's death is concerned. And yet, my heart soars that he was laid to rest under a tree in our village by those who loved him, where I visited him every day until I was brought here in a cattle car, like an animal. My Sandor's tree is not that different from the beautiful tree in the grove that gave us shade and comfort today while we waited. I closed my eyes and imagined I was sitting under his tree. I remembered the child, Gerti, who was with my Sandor when he passed. I thought she must be an angel God sent for him. At his funeral, she whispered to me that throwing dirt on his coffin was like planting a seed that then emerges in a new form. She said she had seen my Sandor's new form and it was beautiful. She put her arms around my neck and in that embrace, passed my son's spirit through me." She paused to remember that moment. "But under this tree, we are lied to, promised a shower and a meal and a place to rest. Instead, we are led to the chamber of agonizing death. So thank you, God, for giving my son the burial he deserved and sparing him this inhumane, ruthless and cruel fate. ..... but I am angry. Please stop the suffering. I'm begging you." Her request to God was her last act before moving on with Gerti, believing that having endured two utterly tragic circumstances somehow gave her special standing to not only ask, but expect that her request would be granted.

Theo summons Gerti to where he and Batya are helping with the spirit transfers. He reminds them that this is only the first group and there are many more to follow, all needing the same care so their spirits can be transported to the World to Come. "I must return to my work with Patti, as she will need me very soon. I leave you to continue the work you have started here. But remember: your mission is to assist the children. They must come first." And with that, he is gone. Batya and Gerti return to the Mother Tree to prepare.

CHAPTER THIRTEEN

Patti met her life partner in her last year of college. They immediately began living together as she was certain of her choice. According to long-ago-made plans, she traveled to New York after graduation to give her Broadway ambitions a chance, but after one short summer, realized it was time to go home. He was home. After four years, they married and had two beautiful boy children. It was only then that the truth became fully available to her.

It was a normal afternoon in their home in Colorado, where they had moved to put physical distance between themselves and her parents. A popular talk show was tackling the bold and some-what controversial subject matter of sexual abuse; identifying it, and daring to talk about it. Every closed pathway in her psyche opened up in a rush as the familiar details were discussed. That initial rush would quickly become a surreal slow- motion slog that lasted for many years.

Armed with what she was certain was the family secret, now uncovered, Patti became a warrior for truth and healing. Naively, she believed that once she led her family through the difficult facts, these facts would be acknowledged, followed by forgiveness and healing. She was exhilarated by the thought of the coming resolution.

No one else in the family seemed at all interested or invested in the truth Patti was seeking. After a short time, all three said they wished she hadn't figured it out and they would prefer things go back to the way they used to be. Patti anticipated this challenge from her parents, but certainly not from her sister. She assumed Kathy had been harmed by their father but had very little understanding of the actual story and how deeply traumatized and fully indoctrinated she was.

But if Kathy and their parents didn't want to pursue it, why should Patti press the matter? What standing did she have? While Patti had escaped the car the night before her sister's wedding, the harm had already been done, even though she couldn't begin to process it until she saw the talk show. Beyond the molestation itself, she began to realize how sexualized their upbringing had been. While the details came into focus, Patti didn't linger on any of them. She had absorbed them throughout her childhood and they were fully a part of her by now. There was no way for her to know the trouble they would eventually cause in her emotional life.

Theo was proud of the work Patti hoped to do with her family but also understood that they would not go along. He knew she would be unsatisfied with anything short of a full healing from the dark stain of abuse that her father had perpetrated on the entire family. But the cost would be very high and the risk would be great.

There would be three men in Patti's story, each playing a key role in her ultimate survival. The story was anchored by her Dutch husband, who was fully formed when she found him at age twenty-four, with a deep intuitive understanding of who she was and where she came from. She knew the first time she saw him she was going to spend the rest of her life with him, if he would have her. She dedicated herself to insuring that outcome. The first time they met, he completely understood her father. He recognized how controlling, how bright, how manipulative, how easily titillated, and how inappropriate he was. It wasn't just a secret fear or an unspoken anxiety for her anymore. Her Dutchman had seen it, seen him, and in so doing, had seen her.

Patti wrote about a subsequent visit by her father.

My father came to visit and insisted on staying with me. I was completely traumatized at the thought of spending the night alone with him in my small apartment. When he first arrived with that familiar grin on his face, he prodded me as to the extent of my sexual relationship with my future husband, his version of a father-daughter talk. He let me know that while my mother should not know about it and would not approve, he did, and it would be our secret. He then asked if I was having regular orgasms, a subject so urgent to him that the conversation took place right away while waiting for his baggage to arrive. I used that opening to tell him that I would be spending the night at the Dutchman's apartment, as I usually did, during his visit. It was odd witnessing his excitement over my new sexual activity while at the same time observing his disappointment that I would not be staying alone with him overnight. I honestly couldn't tell which was more important to him. I imagined his pride in my sexual awakening was similar to what other fathers would feel when their daughters made the honor roll or got a big promotion at work.

Patti's earthly spiritual partner in the story was a gentle soul named Michael. They met in high school, he an artist and she an actress/dancer. She wrote about their first encounter.

He swears it was love at first sight when he looked in the modern dance rehearsal room and saw me dancing on a table, and Michael became the first boy to make me feel safe and loved. He was very careful with me, very patient, and waited in the background when I wanted to experiment with other boys who were starting to occasionally pay attention to me. But he was always there. One day he rang my doorbell with a small box in his hand. It was a promise ring, very dainty with two small diamond chips. I accepted it, wore it on my right hand, and he expected nothing in return. The summer after graduation, my family took a two-week beachfront rental in Myrtle Beach, South Carolina. Michael came to visit for a few days and we spent a carefree, innocent time holding hands, swimming in the ocean, and going to the amusement park in the evenings. When it was time for him to leave, I walked him to his car. Knowing how much he loved me, I was certain that he would speak to the future he envisioned, or at least desperately wanted, for us. I was nervous about it because no matter how comfortable and safe I felt with him, I knew there were many things I would want to accomplish that could not be done with him by my side. He was too sweet, too loving and would not have the stomach for the course my life would inevitably take. It was always hard for him to ask for what he wanted and his strong intuition as to what was best for me was almost always accurate, despite how often it did not include what he wanted for himself. He planned every move carefully. He intuitively knew that if he made any demands on me, asked for any commitments that day at the beach, I would have turned him down. And he was right. Still, he surprised me by asking for nothing. I watched him drive away, knowing he was leaving me to my own future, one that would take place without him, even though that was not what he wanted. Little did I know that he would patiently wait for so many years to re-enter my life and play such a significant part at such a critical time.

The third man could easily have been considered the story's antagonist, were it not for the fact that Patti could not heal herself completely without enormous pain, struggle, and risk. And for that, there was no one more qualified or brilliant for the role than James. He made the pain pleasurable, the struggle seductive, and the risk irresistible. Patti wrote about the first time they met when she was seventeen, a sophomore in college.

He had a sensual, secretive way about him that made you feel as though you were the sole object of his considerable desire and he could not live without having you completely. It started very soon after we became acquainted. He invited me to a hotel room to have his way with me, on a daily basis, and never gave up trying. I was flattered and flustered by this sexual attention, which was completely new to me, as I had never been propositioned before. At seventeen, I certainly wasn't considering his proposition, but imagined I could keep him on the hook at some level without actually having to go all the way which

I had never done and had no intention of doing with him. It was he, for the first time, who made me feel my own sexual power. My father had taught me that a woman's control emanated from her sexuality, but it was never anything I could believe or relate to. Until James. Day after day, he turned every comment into a sexual image, an invitation, a summons. What I don't think he counted on was that we would get to know each other and become close friends. His other relationships were hunt, conquer, and leave. Although I was certainly hunted, I wasn't about to be conquered, and he wasn't leaving.

How could she have known at the time that his persistent long-term pursuit of her would lead directly to the most dangerous threat she would ever face, but would also create such a lifesaving and profound opportunity for transformative healing?

Theo allowed the curtain to come up on Patti's life play where her searching monologues would take place: each player would perform their part brilliantly, and after a dramatic climax, the story would resolve. Then, and only then, would Patti be able to play her role in the spirit mission.

CHAPTER FOURTEEN

By now the children and their families were coming into the grove in waves, staying a short while before being moved to the killing facility down the path where they were forced to take off their clothes prior to being herded into the gas chamber, a humiliating ritual. Bodies were removed from the chamber and shaved after death was achieved and a full search was conducted to remove any valuable materials from teeth or other body parts. The hair was processed, batched and sold as industrial raw material in Germany.

Batya and Gerti initiated their work during the short waiting period in the grove when the groups were calm, believing they were going to be showered and fed soon. Batya danced through the grove to uplift and prepare the children for what was to come. She threw blankets of light and sparkle over the pathway to death and created a special space for each child. Gerti, positioned in the Mother Tree, poured buckets of stars below and was ready to usher the children to the light after Batya sent them her way. They used their spirit powers to intensify the sensation of love their families felt for them so those would be the last powerful emotions experienced by all, loving and being loved, prior to the sheer terror of such a cruel shared demise.

Children usually transition more easily because they have fewer earthly experiences to process. But because of the level of trauma in the way they died, many of the child spirits, especially the girls, became very attached to Batya and her warm, ethereal beauty and did not want to leave her. Batya individually assisted those particular children, slowly coaxing them to move towards Gerti and the light portal. But they clung to Batya. And each child took a little piece of her beautiful tender spirit with them as they finally let go and trusted Gerti with the last part of their short journey.

And they kept coming. One transport after another. 200,000 children in fifty-six days. Although spirits are multi-dimensional and do not experience linear time as do humans, the overwhelming sense of the assigned mission, and the unexpected complexity of the work with the young spirits, caused Batya to tire. Gerti tried to care for her when possible and saw the toll the work was taking on her. But they kept going.

Sometimes the adult spirits crowded the space with their sheer volume. Very few of them were ready to go. They had so many powerful, complex emotions to process. It was difficult for Gerti and Batya to continue to concentrate exclusively on the children when so many others needed their help. But they followed the mission. And the transports kept coming. Over 3,000 Hungarian Jews every day, sometimes twice a day, almost half of them children.

CHAPTER FIFTEEN

Patti's psychic fracture began slowly, like foreshocks of an earthquake. She had allowed James to become a regular part of her life but it was a dangerous game. As a young woman of considerable integrity, proud of her family life and professional accomplishments, she could never dream of such behavior. But the way she responded to his attention and to his touch when she allowed it, was like a drug. The stronger her growing need, the wider the fracture grew. There was no way to explain what came over her when she indulged her addiction as it was completely out of character. All she knew was that it felt familiar in an interior way, as though she were fulfilling some type of dark prophecy.

The unbearable pain of existing in this new world of secrecy and shame took its toll. She couldn't consciously understand what she was doing, but she couldn't stop doing it. She rarely stopped writing, as a pure survival mechanism, often in the middle of the night when her family was sleeping.

I never feel well anymore. I doubt I have a disease, at least not one of the medically diagnosable type. Perhaps a social disease. A physical social disease. My state of mind began affecting my health when I was ten-years-old, and my ability to carry the pain of others is something I have always had trouble controlling. I'm not ten anymore, but my illnesses are still undiagnosable. My head aches. My muscles feel like bricks. My stomach hurts. I look awful. I don't sleep because I have my episodes in the middle of the night. Trying to diagnose the undiagnosable illness. By now the energy is all gone and only the brain remains active. That contributes to the undiagnosable nature of the problem. Worn out, beat down, you think about those people whose problems are much worse than yours and they have experienced a triumph of the human spirit. But their problems were so diagnosable, like cancer or being shot or paralyzed. It's cleaner somehow. Me, I just cry when I think about my sister's emotional wounds that have left her in so much pain and so alone that she can barely function. I think about how I am destroying such a beautiful life with no idea why. And I continue.

Patti's father had continually educated her by promoting his disturbed philosophy on everything from current events to his perceived assumed expertise on human behavior. He declared there was no such thing as rape, because all women wanted it. As a result, there was always consent. He and Patti's mother thrived on the Anita Hill-Clarence Thomas hearings, repeatedly vilifying the woman who made those "ridiculous accusations" against the judge who was, after all, "just being a man." They were ecstatic when she was "put in her place where she belonged" and the judge was confirmed to the Supreme Court. Her father privately explained to Patti that the Navy's Tail Hook scandal justified his own behaviors with his "fighter pilots will be fighter pilots" philosophy, stating proudly, "It's just the way we are. No big deal. I'm no different than them." Patti made the distinction that, while those pilots may see their female counterparts in a sexual way and inappropriately act on it, as they did at Tail Hook, it is unlikely that their chauvinistic attitudes of entitlement extended to sexual contact with their daughters.

She continued to write, internal monologues, that she prayed would lead her out of this miserable existence.

My father had taught me, by example, how to use every ounce of my intelligence to control, manipulate, and prevail in every situation. I had learned my lesson so well that I eventually became better at it than him, ultimately gaining the very control that had once been his evil weapon against us. I was struck by the similarities between James and my father, both powerful and controlling, leading a secret life and totally believing they somehow had the right. My father once told me that he did not think he had hurt his family by having his secret life because he was still a good husband, good provider, and good father. But he had the need and capacity to have more. I was totally disgusted by his selfish ravings at the time, hating him for deciding what did and didn't hurt our family, what did and didn't destroy our mother, what did and didn't cause him to treat my sister like a mistress. And here I was now, involved with a man just like him in so many ways: myself being the other woman, being the potential cause of so much hurt and shame. I began to believe that I was just like him, as my mother had told me on more than one occasion, and became determined to prove it. I felt completely worthless and filled with self-loathing.

Her Dutch husband understood that something was terribly wrong. Sometimes Patti would cry uncontrollably while unable to explain herself to him. He never asked her to. He knew she had to go through it, whatever it was, and hoped she would figure it out before she destroyed herself—and their family. She was overwhelmed with love for him and knew that he was the difference between barely managing each day and losing everything. She knew what she had to do, but didn't know if she could.

CHAPTER SIXTEEN

From her perch in the grove's Mother Tree, Gerti senses that the group of Hungarian families below is the last. Batya is dancing amongst the children, encouraging them to play and smile, and making sure they feel loved. Gerti's stars seem bigger than usual, and when she tips over a bucket, they last longer in the air. As she joins Batya below, the guard arrives and instructs everyone to begin moving down the path. With one graceful toss, Batya lays down her blanket of light along the path for all the children, and Gerti helps shepherd them to the crematorium facility. After they are forced to undress, the spirits accompany them into the chamber as the families finally realize that this is not a shower and they will never have the meal they were promised. Once death has been achieved, the children's spirits immediately begin to leave their physical bodies. Batya greets each one and gently leads them to Gerti who awaits at the tunnel of light where they transition. As the last child slips through the tunnel, there is, for the first time, a sense of stillness. Not because there aren't active spirits— because there are more adult spirits than could be counted or processed at that time—but because there are no more children. All of the Hungarian Jewish children have left the earth. Gerti and Batya come together in a spirit embrace that is so profound that they nearly become one. They return to the grove and the loving embrace of the Mother Tree that has been witness to every moment of their sacred work. The two spirits fall into a deep, rejuvenating state.

They are roused by the strong and active spirit of an old woman. Gerti recognizes her from the bakery in her village. The old woman is agitated and states that after wandering aimlessly in her spirit state for what seems like an eternity, she is finally in need of processing and asks for their help. They approach her and offer encouragement. Her face is still wrenched in pain, and clearly it is very difficult for her to finally let go of her story.

"We lived a quiet life in the village before all this happened. I had two daughters and one young grandson, eighteen-months-old. I loved being a grandmother. Who wouldn't? No one understood what was happening to us. There were whispers but some things were just too terrible to believe. We were forced to give up our businesses, leave our homes, live in a ghetto, and then ride on a train meant not for humans for three days and nights, standing up the whole way because there was no room to sit. No water, no food. People dying around us. One small window our only light. When the train finally stopped, it took a while before they unlocked the car from the outside. The light streamed in, hurting our eyes. There were guards with dogs and they yelled at us to get out. Some were pulled to the ground. People were being put in lines but we didn't know where we were or why, much less where these lines might lead. Prisoners in striped uniforms were helping the guards. One of them came close to me and whispered that any person carrying a child would be sent to their death right away. Strong young people would be put to work. If this prisoner had been caught talking to me, he would have been shot immediately. I knew what this meant. Women and their children and people too old to work would not survive this day. I went to my younger daughter who was holding her small frightened child and told her that I had learned that the older people and the young children were treated the best at this place so she should give the child to me so we could be cared for together. She began to resist, but before she could, my young grandson was already in my arms. I gently pushed my daughter towards her older sister, knowing they would be chosen for work and would have each other. My grandson and I joined the line with the mothers, grandmothers, children, and elders. I looked over my shoulder and yelled out to my older daughter to take care of her sister. I knew how much care she would require when she realized her own mother had lied to her. Her own mother had prevented her from choosing whether to die with her child. I'm a mother, too. And today my daughter is not dead...like we are. I feel so much guilt for lying to my daughter and making that choice for her. How can she ever forgive me? How can I ever forgive myself?"

She is wailing while Batya and Gerti envelop her in their loving energy, letting her know it is good to let go and leave for the World to Come. They remind her that her young grandson is waiting for her. Rather than taking her to the portal of light, they form an energy circle around her, empowering her to create her own light source. She slowly begins to rise out of the arms of the two spirits, although her ongoing natural resistance causes an unusual delay in her progress. Batya requests assistance from the spirits above and they reach down and pull the old woman up. As she rises, her form is laid out with the agony of her disclosure. As she progresses, she becomes lighter, and lighter, until she reaches the World to Come. Her pain is extinguished.

CHAPTER SEVENTEEN

IF THE WRONGNESS of Patti's continuing involvement with James was a descent of the flesh, reconnecting with Michael was an ascension of the spirit. He was a tender soul, quiet and patient and resolute in his unconditional care for her. Not being in touch for a long while had not stopped him from continuing to nurture their connection. Patti had always felt that, a sense of being old and familiar, now ready to move forward, brought to a higher level, built on trust established long ago. Their ability to communicate and experience each other did not require physical proximity, which they did not have. Michael made sure that their connection was clean, never tainted, no matter what his personal feelings may be.

They wrote to one another and, after a few letters, she disclosed the sexual abuse that was in complete control of her life at that moment. He became her living journal, a safe place to share the difficult feelings of shame and confusion that were her everyday companions. Being an artist, he made their interaction beautiful by way of lyrical words, lovely handwriting, drawings and paintings. She wasn't in love with him, but loved him deeply for his ability to understand her pain and soothe her aching soul.

She was still leading two separate lives. The part that was experimenting and struggling with the long-term impact of having been raised on sex was becoming more and more detached from reality. Michael was a light-filled space, a safe haven, a hopeful influence. How bad could she be if such a good person held such a place of love for her? He never judged her harshly when she confessed her shocking behavior, but worried about her constantly. She became better and better at disassociating from the behavior, compartmentalizing all of it more and more, like an out of body experience that had everything to do with her body.

She wrote to Michael, "I feel as bad physically as I can ever remember without actually being sick. You appeared to me in a very vivid dream. You didn't walk into the room, instead, you kind of floated in slow motion while all the others of us walked normally. You were surrounded by a warm but strong light. I didn't seem to be expecting you, but when I saw you, I was filled with joy. I know that this dream was your way of trying to protect me and help me believe in the goodness of me. But I'm a tough case, you know. In some ways, I think I've had a bit of a mini-nervous breakdown. Instead of being hospitalized—and I've prayed for that—I am going to God's natural hospital, the shore. Today I feel as though I have risen above myself and am looking down on me. Almost like being dead in a way, I imagine."

In response, Michael wrote, "I am beginning to sense the duality that drives you and concerns you. Go away to whatever place or space in life's drama that is needed. No, demanded, because without it you will die little bits at a time inside. I'm afraid of the little cracks becoming fractures. I don't know yet if any of us close to you have the alchemy to mix the ointment in order to heal the cracks before they widen."

CHAPTER EIGHTEEN

Theo arrives in the grove to check on his sprits, knowing they have completed their mission. He lands in the lower branches of the Mother Tree, under which Batya and Gerti are resting, still trying to rejuvenate. He gazes at them for a moment, understanding the enormous task they completed, proud of their work. With a small gesture, he awakens them and they immediately understand he is present. They look up at him with reverence. In a slightly stern voice, somewhat teasing, he says, "I see you are still here. And yet your mission is over. All the children are gone. Their souls have been delivered. You did that."

Batya quietly steps forward with deep respect and struggles to express herself verbally, which she does only when absolutely necessary. "It is true that all the children have been delivered. But so many other spirits remain, with so much to do before they can leave this place. They haven't let go of their anger, their confusion, their doubt, their loved ones. So they linger. How can we leave while they remain?" She bows her head to Theo and continues, "I know it is beyond the scope of our mission for the children...." She reaches her hand out to Gerti who joins her in the sacred request. "We ask permission to continue."

Theo takes note of the obvious shared state of the two spirits and moves his gaze to Gerti who drops her head, knowing that Theo could end her time in the grove in an instant. He addresses Batya, "What about this little one?" he says, gesturing to Gerti.

Batya responds, "She has become a powerful but gentle presence for this difficult work. And very well suited to it. In order to continue, I will need her help."

"And what about you, little one?" Theo asks, gazing down at Gerti. "What do you want?"

"I want very much to stay with Batya" she answers shyly, eyes cast down.

Theo responds in a serious and foreboding tone, addressing Batya, "You know this will be very difficult. And it may not go as you imagine." Batya nods and repeats her request, "We cannot leave them behind. We cannot leave them. We must help them find their way out."

"Very well then," Theo concedes. "I ordain this grove for your continuing work." With that, he slowly raises his arms toward his spirits, closes his eyes, and confers a blessing upon them. "You may rely on this beautiful and powerful Mother Tree for shelter, safety, comfort and wisdom. And so I leave you, Batya, and you, child. Bless you. Bless you both." And he evaporates from his space in the Mother Tree, knowing the trauma he is leaving behind. He knows that Batya is not well and this additional element to the original mission will cause her demise. But he also knows that Gerti has become a profoundly strong spirit in her own right. She will finish the work herself, but will require assistance to make her own exit. He will make sure that Patti is ready when Gerti needs her. For now, she is on her own mission.

CHAPTER NINETEEN

Patti's Dutch husband continues his unconditional support, a kind of safe anchor that she cannot believe that he still provides and certainly knows she doesn't deserve. She hangs on to it for dear life and hopes that she can find her way out before he has had enough. He still doesn't know specifically what she is going through, but knows it is essential and is willing to accept that for now.

One particular day, her agitation level is significant. The Dutchman tells her gently that if she is not careful, she will put all of her terrible stress into a tumor and he knows she is capable of doing so. She understands it is meant as a warning, but something in her stirs and it is taken as a suggestion. Not consciously, but stored in an accessible space.

She knows she needs help and considers her decision to approach her parents' therapist a positive step. He knows he should not treat her due to the obvious conflict, but she convinces him that she is in crisis and doesn't have time to start from the beginning of the story with someone else. She understands that he cannot discuss anything from their sessions, but at least he knows them, who they are—and that means everything at this moment. He reluctantly agrees, knowing he is on shaky ethical ground.

She tells him the truth about James and her inability to act on his perpetual invitation or walk away. As a consequence, she has agreed to meet James in two days when she will go through with what she has been avoiding for so long, because she knows she deserves it. She no longer believes she is worthy of her husband, children, or self-esteem. She must declare who she really is, and was raised to be, and prove that she is "just like him." She begins to cry from the sheer agony of the declaration. He offers a box of tissues and a sharp rebuke, stating that the decision will ruin her life and make her a permanent victim of the abuse. He wonders how she would ever consciously choose to be so self-destructive. She has no answer. And he doesn't have one that can stop her.

Theo is present when Patti and James meet in a small, dark hotel room. While he has made it a point not to interfere with the story she is living, he wants to protect her, should it be too difficult for her to reclaim herself when the moment comes. Patti intends to proceed but when James is ready for her, she reaches as deeply as she can inside herself and refuses to continue. There is absolutely no connection between them, which is what makes it easier and what makes it so devastating. He is not kind. He departs. It is over.

Theo stays close as Patti stands in the middle of the now empty room while the essence of her drops through her entire body down to the tips of her toes, like a robe slipping from her shoulders, completely emptying her inside. At that moment, she forms her disease, instantly beginning to create the tumor, a mass that will encompass all her pain and suffering and abuse and lust and self-loathing. All of those emotions begin a rush to her breast, the breast where her father first touched her, and where she symbolically places her tumor.

She somehow manages to save herself in that dreary hotel room by finally rejecting her own version of her father's daughter and by rejecting James who may as well have been her father by this time. Her knees are like water as she struggles to put on her shoes and actually walk out the door. In her state, she doesn't recognize salvation.

CHAPTER TWENTY

It was true that Batya's request to extend the mission to the adult spirits was more difficult than she imagined. There were more of them and their transitions were far more time-consuming and complex. The spirits had been wandering a while; and the longer they stayed without departing, the harder it was to leave. Batya began losing her own shape and taking on theirs, her pale spirit light dimming and the extra weight of her duty exhausting her. Now as she attempted to dance through the spirit field, her movement became desolate. And still she gave her all to assist the spirits that were ready to move on. Theo intervened to grant her additional strength. But in that she was not generating it herself, it was temporary.

Gerti was torn between devoting herself to her spirit sister and continuing on with the work they had convinced Theo they were prepared to do. She had learned how to intuit the issues of each spirit that delayed or prevented transition and form them into like groups so they could encourage each other to move on. This helped things go along more quickly and eased the guilty burden Batya felt for not being more productive. As her spirit light dimmed, Gerti's grew brighter. She was becoming more efficient in helping the spirits depart, and while there was still much work to do, she believed she could finish the extended mission on her own. Gerti delivered Batya to the largest branch of the Mother Tree where she could rest and oversee the work, hoping they could stay together long enough to see the last of the spirits depart.

CHAPTER TWENTY-ONE

Knowing what she has done, Patti continues to write to come to terms with her present situation. It is startlingly clear.

Within three days, the tumor I made appears in my right breast. It isn't subtle. There are knots and lumps, and it is hot and swollen. I go to my gynecologist who says I should watch it for thirty days. So I watch my cancer thrive unattended and buy the next bra size to accommodate its rapid growth. I lay frozen peas on it to lower its temperature. When I return to the doctor, he views the tumor, backs away, and says I must see the surgeon, now. The surgeon opens the gown and walks backwards all the way across the room. How powerful my tumor must be to make doctors retreat. An immediate biopsy is scheduled. I refuse general anesthesia and am wheeled into a cold operating room with a heavy cloth across my face. I hear the surgeon enter, but no one tells him I am wide awake and fully conscious under my blue sheet. He seems surprised at the tumor's appearance and opts for an immediate frozen section rather than the original plan to wait twenty-four hours for routine lab results. The call comes in with the results and he returns to the table, saying nothing. I ask, "Is it benign?" He is shocked to hear my voice from under the blue drape. He says simply, "no." At first I feel overwhelming relief, spontaneous and consuming. Then a very powerful, spiritual presence folds me in its aura, giving me an immediate sense of peace. And faith, a very real thing, presents itself, filling me with the belief that I will get sick to get well. Completely well from the sickness of my life. I will heal myself. This will be my story.

pneuma

CHAPTER TWENTY-TWO

THEO ROSE to the position of supreme leader of the Spirit Council because he had the will and the stamina to provide assistance to those who were in various stages of transition. He also had a unique and rare talent for divining the spirit issues of others. He identified those who would be suited to work for him as well as those who were not capable of long-term service and would continue to seek a way out. He always knew who was ready to move on, who needed more time and why, and who had the psychological endurance to make a career as a long-term spirit.

In addition to determining which missions would be established, Theo was charged with identifying humans who, in the midst of mortal lives on earth, were already in tune with the spirit world. This could take the form of being asked to assist spirits who needed help transitioning, the kind of permission sometimes only a human could give.

By the time she was a young woman, Patti had experienced these spirit requests. In one such case, a twenty-three-year-old woman, a close family friend, died on her last run down a snow-covered Colorado mountain at sunset. She was killed instantly, although there was barely a mark on her body. She had contacted her mother just moments before the fateful run with a message of love. The mother later told Patti that she always knew her only daughter would not spend a full lifetime on earth and was not surprised by her sudden departure in such a peaceful way. The ability of loved ones to come to know such things are part of the human help that provides pathways between spirit and family.

Patti was asked to make a video to be shared at the celebration of life service. The photos were left at the funeral home where Patti went to collect them. When she entered, the spirit of the young woman completely filled the space, literally flying around, full of energy. Patti felt so welcomed by this vibrant spirit that she delayed her departure so she could spend more time with her. She took the photos home, dozens of them taken at all stages of her adventurous life around the world. The parents had provided one, framed, of her in a beautiful white ball gown. That was the one Patti put on her work desk, the one that kept her company while fulfilling the sacred responsibility of representing such a beautiful life to her many friends and family. Exhausted, Patti finally finished the work and went to bed the night before the upcoming service.

At 2:35 a.m., she was awakened from a deep sleep to see the young woman at her bedside. She was floating in a translucent white dress, the spirit version of the one she wore in the photo. She looked completely at ease and expressed her gratitude and friendship by reaching out to actually touch Patti's cheek. This unusual physical contact defined a spirit that did not need assistance in transitioning; she was saying good-bye.

Patti returned the photos to the family shortly after the service, but did not include the framed photo she had kept on her desk because she was not yet ready to part with it, to part with the profound experience they had shared. Weeks later she returned the photo to her parents and told them of her experience with their daughter's beautiful spirit in the days immediately following her death. It was difficult for Patti to part with it, but she knew better than to be an impediment to a near perfect transition. She must let go with the same grace as the wise young spirit who departed in peace and left only gratitude behind.

CHAPTER TWENTY-THREE

It was all well and good that Patti saw her self-invented tumor as a direct path to healing, but Theo knew that path would not be smooth. Her first visit with the doctor that he selected would be crucial to her belief that the physical was deeply linked to the spiritual. She had done well managing to get this far along in her healing with very little direct help from Theo. But now that her medical situation was so threatening, he decided to inhabit the doctor for the initial visit, just as he had when she was a young girl calling for her father to help understand why her classmate's paralysis had become her own. It was essential that fear and panic did not overshadow Patti's connection to the greater mission at hand.

He reached out his hand to hers and said, "Good afternoon. Sorry to keep you waiting."

"Have we met before? You seem familiar to me." said Patti, studying his face.

"No, I don't believe so," he said smiling warmly. "Please sit down. Your tests are back. Our estimate is that your breast tumor is very large and growing rapidly." His voice was serious but calm, confident and reassuring. "It's a mass actually, eleven centimeters," he said, his sweet cadence belying the gravity of the content. "As a result, it is likely that you have significant lymph node involvement as well. If you have more than ten cancerous nodes, we will consider a stem cell rescue, a type of bone marrow transplant. If your stem cells are cancer free, you can donate them to yourself which makes the process less risky and more likely to succeed."

Patti immediately recognized that this was potentially what she had been trying to orchestrate. She was not fearful or upset. "How does it work?"

"Four rounds of outpatient chemotherapy to begin. If you qualify, you donate your own stem cells and they are immediately frozen. You check into the transplant unit at the hospital and take up residence in a sterile room. You are given four kinds of high dose chemo for four days in a non-stop drip to kill your compromised immune system, leaving you with a feeling of being completely empty inside. When you are at your lowest point, we infuse you with your healthy stem cells."

Interrupting him, "So you are saying that I will kill my compromised immune system with high dose chemo and when my immune system is completely burned out, along with whatever else I choose to burn out of me, I will receive my own stem cells back in my sterile room. Then I will make every cell in my body from scratch?"

"Yes, exactly, Patti. We think of it as a rebirth. In fact, I like to hold a christening ceremony on the day your stem cells are infused, complete with the white dress."

She looked upward and clasped her hands as if thanking God for answering her prayer, "Yes, absolutely. I want that. I will rebirth myself....by myself. In a sterile room."

"But first we have to get that tumor out. Right away." He changed his tone and says, "I have to say that most people don't consider this good news. And want no part of it. But not you. Why is that, Patti?" he asked, gazing at her with pride, knowing the answer.

"I made this tumor myself," she said, placing her hand on her chest, taking ownership of the large, visible mass. "And it is filled with some very old and dark things that I tried many other ways to overcome. None of them worked. I knew I needed something more powerful to get rid of what has been growing inside of me, that now has shape and form. I placed it all in this tumor in the hopes that it could be removed...before it killed me. I never dreamed of the type of procedure you are describing. A true physical and spiritual rebirth. A prayer answered."

"Obviously you have some serious things to accomplish through this process. Leave the science to me. And you take care of the part that only you can do for yourself. Parallel paths. Same outcome: a new life." He tempers that commitment with a reminder of the seriousness of what she is about to undertake. "Patti, you know this will be very difficult and it may not go as you imagine."

"I understand. And I am willing to take the risk. I must."

"Very well then," he said as he placed his hands on her shoulders, looking directly into her eyes. "We will do this together. And sooner rather than later. My office will call to get everything set up."

Patti found herself praying that her tumor was just dangerous enough to have infected more than ten lymph nodes so she could qualify for the stem cell rescue.

CHAPTER TWENTY-FOUR

When Theo returned to the top of the grove's Mother Tree, he saw the fear and despair in Gerti's young face when she looked up at him. She was watching over Batya, whose pale spirit light was now a dull grey and nearly extinguished. But he did notice that there were many fewer adult spirits roaming the grove than last time. Knowing that was mostly Gerti's doing, he also knew that she always arranged for Batya to participate in some way, no matter how small a contribution she could manage. He called to Gerti to join him in his branch atop the still strong but now painfully delicate birch tree. The grove proceedings had taken a toll on her as well. Gerti had never been allowed on Theo's branch, but he felt she deserved it for the magnificent spirit work she was doing in her own right. He comforted her in his beautiful aura as he explained that it was time for Batya to join the others in the World to Come. He asked if she would she like to assist with the ascension ceremony. Gerti nodded her head yes.

They descended to the clearing in the grove. Theo "spoke" to Gerti non-verbally, directing her to a space between two trees. She knew where she belonged, facing away from Theo and Batya, who was now draped in his arms. Gerti sensed a disturbance behind her, but knew not to look. Instead, she faced the breeze, stood perfectly still, and closed her tired eyes, allowing the heavenly air to soothe her. The disturbance became more active, whipping up a whirlwind. It reached an energy climax and shot off like a rocket into the sky through the small clearing of branches. And then it was absolutely calm and peaceful, quiet and still.

The adult spirits had kept their distance, hovering in a motionless mass as they witnessed their beloved Batya depart. Gerti encouraged them to join her in the empty space where Batya and Theo had been, knowing that when they did, they would discover they had stayed long enough and would follow Gerti to the light. There they would find their children, their parents, their grandparents and Batya. Gerti threw the last blanket of light and sparkle to guide the procession of remaining spirits, just as Batya had for their children and grandchildren. She stood at the entrance to the World to Come and gently sent them off individually until she was the only spirit left in the grove. She curled up in the crook of a branch in the Mother Tree.

CHAPTER TWENTY-FIVE

Patti lies in her hospital bed in the transplant unit. She has the corner room with windows on two walls where she can look down three stories and see the world proceeding without her. Cars, joggers in the park, hospital workers and visitors coming and going. But none of it has anything to do with her. They say you enter and leave this world alone, no matter how many others take part in your arrival and departure. Patti decides to add bone marrow transplant to the list because it happens to you and you alone despite the engagement of friends, family, and medical personnel who truly care for you. It is very isolating.

The four outpatient chemo treatments had been difficult to manage. Until the tenth day after infusion, the sickness was overwhelming. She continually reminded herself that the symptoms are related to treatment, not the disease itself. She was required to take injections each day during the chemo cycles to keep her white cell counts up. Her husband administered the shots, one day in her thigh, another in her stomach, depending on where she could tolerate them. After the shots, Patti's bones buzzed as her white cells proliferated. The doctor said he had never heard of anyone being consciously aware of that process. It is hard for Patti to imagine not being consciously aware of it.

One day, weeks after tearfully allowing her hairdresser to cut short her trademark long hair, she took off her bucket hat and what was left of her hair was in it. She cried like a baby and locked herself in the bathroom, inviting only her older son in to see what was happening. He coaxed her out to see her husband holding the razor he used to buzz the boys' hair. He buzzed what was left of hers. They all took turns rubbing her bald head and kindly exclaiming how good it felt and how chic she looked. Still, it was shocking to have it gone, and she felt incredibly scared and completely exposed.

The collection of her clean stem cells took place over four days. The team said she was the most prolific donor they had ever seen. But it was exhausting. At one point, they couldn't find a blood pressure. The cells went off to the freezer facility where they would stay until she was ready to receive them back. There was a lot of work to do before that could happen. She was grateful that she could donate to herself.

Now her transplant room is always filled with music, mostly classical, sometimes mystical, and all who enter seem spellbound by the palpable energy that fills Patti's sterile space. She controls the temperature, the humidity, and no one can directly breathe the rarified air but her. All visitors are masked and gowned.

It takes over 10 ten days for her cells to bottom out after the high dose chemo and it is filled with physical, mental, and spiritual misery. She writes when she can.

Sometimes it's hard to believe as I endure this experience that it is leading to anything but the grave. I often feel I am lying on the edge of death waiting to be pulled back. The fear, of course, is that I won't come back.

She picks up a mirror to see what the reflection has to say and speaks her monologue of truth out loud. "This all seemed so simple when I first imagined it. Get sick to get well. Place a tumor where my trauma was born and burn out that trauma. But this is so hard. My energy continues to drain out of me and there is nothing left. Sometimes I want to stop working so hard, and just turn my head on the pillow, close my eyes, and let go."

Theo has been with her much of the time. He knows she is

in jeopardy and must intervene. While she sleeps, he lifts his arms and the room turns a strange twilight grey. A large Blue Dragonfly Queen appears, an exquisite creature with a magnificent wingspan wrapped in a cocoon of stretchy blue mesh that makes the perfect place for Patti to nestle when she needs strength, comfort, and emotional shelter. The Queen is joined by the Black Guard, dragonflies dressed in goggles and leather jackets, buzzing around at high speed, in formation, sounding like a hive of bees. Finally, the Golden Dragonfly Troupe appears, tiny and very young dragonflies wearing gold tutus, sparkling as they try to dance, but mostly giggling and careening into one another as they lose their balance and fall into a heap. Theo exclaims to Patti's subconscious, "Here is your Blue Dragonfly Queen. When you need her protection and strength, simply crawl into her. She will live inside of you. The Black Guard will fight cancer cells in your body and the cells will be no match for them. The Golden Dragonfly Troupe will remind you of your brand-new start. Not so different from when you were a tiny ballerina yourself. They are here for you now so when you awake, you will know that you are not alone, Patti. We are with you...and there is work to be done!" Theo retreats. Patti sleeps deeply.

A young woman slips quietly into the room, fully masked and gowned. She sees that Patti is sleeping, so she gently pulls up a chair beside her bed. Nikki is Patti's massage therapist, a dear friend who has provided deep spiritual and physical relief since the diagnosis, and one of the few people that Patti has agreed to see during the dark days of the transplant. She reaches for Patti's hand and holds it with both of hers, closing her eyes, and entering into a deep meditative state. When Nikki opens her eyes, she can see the Blue Dragonfly Queen, the Black Guard and the Golden Dragonfly Troupe. She slowly stands, moving to the center of the room to take in the spectacular display, pleased because she knows that they are Patti's personal healing symbols and deeply moved by the opportunity to witness them before they become a part of Patti's interior life.

Patti stirs and Nikki returns to her side. "Nikki! I had the most amazing dream. I was feeling so low and sick and discouraged when I drifted off. Then I saw...." She sees the images throughout her room and sits up in her bed, breathless with joy.

Nikki responds, "I know. I see them, too!" The images begin to fade as Patti breathes in full deep breaths, inhaling the healing community of dragonflies created for her benefit. "Let me help you," Nikki says, as she carefully tucks Patti back into bed. "I brought you something."

Patti smiles and carefully unwraps the blue package. In it is a dazzling crystal dragonfly on a string, reflecting multiple colors in the light. Patti cups it in her hands and holds it to her chest. "How did you know?!!" They share an embrace. Words aren't needed.

CHAPTER TWENTY-SIX

With Theo's quiet assistance, Patti and Gerti began the slow process of nurturing themselves back to full strength. It was a time of contemplation as they each tried to come to terms with their past experiences and how they translated to the future.

Gerti had come into her spirit powers differently than the others. She was the only one who was not born human followed by a human death. Batya had created Gerti of herself and, with the help of her fellow spirits, embedded her in the womb of a Hungarian Jew, just a short while before all Hungarian Jews would be transported to Auschwitz/Birkenau. Gerti lived as a human throughout the time spent with her family and their friends and neighbors, including dying with them in the gas chamber, but she was always a spirit.

Theo allowed Gerti and Patti to discover what the future held at their own pace. But the gift of intuition that both possessed helped them not only process what was happening, but provided the insight as to how best to use their abilities to transcend the trauma that surrounded them.

The toll it took was great. Patti had invited a vicious disease to enter her body as a way to burn out her past and rebirth herself. She would live the rest of her life with those scars, but had accomplished her goal. Gerti had borne witness to one of the greatest atrocities in human history at a breathtaking pace, and worked at an equal pace to guard the souls of the children, and then their families, in order to insure that they would not get trapped in the death camp.

In that one was human and one spirit, they recovered in different ways. Patti was thrust back into the world, full of real responsibilities and relationships. Gerti stayed in her state of spiritual suspension, nestled in the grove's Mother Tree, experiencing the process internally. Patti's recovery was measured in real time, day in and day out. For Gerti, time did not exist.

CHAPTER TWENTY-SEVEN

Patti's re-entry to life was not as easy as she imagined. Yes, she was clean, unburdened by the weight of her painful past, but it was a life she did not at all recognize. She poured her energy into reclaiming her place with her family, her business, and herself. A friend recommended a therapist who could assist her in discovering what this new life might look and feel like. On their first meeting, she told Patti that during her morning meditation, she had seen her in the forest surrounded by dragonflies. By this time, Patti was well inhabited by the dragonflies that Theo had gifted her. The Blue Dragonfly Queen was a source of constant motherly and spiritual comfort; the Black Guard patrolled her bloodstream to deter any cancer cells; and the Golden Dragonfly Troupe of tiny dancers reminded her of the joy that she now believed she deserved in her life.

Patti took a road trip to the beach with two dear friends from her childhood. While passing through a beautiful forest, they stopped for gas at a small rural station with two old-fashioned pumps. As she headed to the small structure to pay for the gas, Patti found herself suddenly surrounded by a huge swarm of dragonflies, hundreds of them. She commented to the older gentleman at the cash register that the station must be in a dragonfly corridor for so many to be coming through at once. He looked at her oddly and said "Lady, I've worked here for thirty years, and have never seen a dragonfly once in that entire time."

She spent most of her time with the therapist learning how to connect to a world outside of her everyday existence, exploring her intuitive and spiritual abilities and what part they would play in her new life. This created a peace inside of her that had been impossible to access in her former life. She gradually discovered that it was perfectly fine to exist in that precious space, without doing anything, or accomplishing anything, other than being present.

Patti visited Sedona, Arizona through a program that introduced her to a number of practitioners and therapists known for their work in the spiritual realm. While much of it was focused on healing, which Patti had done on a grand scale through her bone marrow transplant and rebirth, she was more interested in learning how to incorporate the practices into everyday life. It was there that she met her new teacher and spiritual mentor, who immediately recognized Patti's potential for spirit work and helped her tune in to those abilities. She taught Patti to trust in what she knew to be true but was sometimes afraid to accept and believe.

At a follow-up medical appointment, Patti ran into one of her transplant nurses who was thrilled to see her full head of new curly hair. Patti said she wasn't sure if the nurse remembered her, but she was filled with gratitude for the care and companionship provided by all the nurses during her weeks in the transplant unit. The nurse said, "Are you kidding? We all remember you! We didn't know what was going on in your room, but whatever it was, we all wanted to be in there." "Healing," Patti said. "It was healing."

CHAPTER TWENTY-EIGHT

Gerti awakened to her new reality. She was still in the grove's Mother Tree, refreshed from her deep rest but with many questions. Theo observed from high above, knowing that Gerti had a lot to wrestle with and also knowing that it wasn't time for him to step in—or even make his presence known to her. This contemplative work must be done by herself, for herself.

It was hard for Gerti to understand who she was and all that she had been through during her time in Hungary and later in what seemed to be the endless job of assisting spirits in exiting the dreadful, notorious killing camp. But now, at this moment, it was just a beautiful birch grove where sometimes the trees blew softly in the breeze and sometimes the branches drooped under the weight of the winter snowfall, with no visible signs of the unimaginable horror of the past. But the trees had witnessed everything; and they knew, just as Gerti did, what happened there. For now, they were her only companions.

She allowed herself to feel the memory of her time in Hungary, the love of her grandmother, the closeness with her sister, the joy of playing with the neighborhood boys, and the tenderness she felt towards her father. She thought about the night she had been awakened by a dark, foreboding dream and hugged herself in the chill of the night as she stood at the small bedroom window in the light of the moon. In the far, far distance, she had seen a chimney with flames licking out the top, not knowing if it was real or if she was still dreaming. She had asked God if it was just a bad dream. He didn't answer.

She knew she wasn't a human like the others; but some of the time, she felt like one. There were moments when she was aware of her spirit powers. When Sandor died in the street, she knew she had the ability to bring him back to life. At the time, she didn't understand why Batya refused to allow her to do that, instead saying that one day she would understand why. Now she did understand that at least one child should be afforded the burial any child deserved, honored by the community and laid to rest under a beautiful old tree. The remaining children would all die in the gas chamber. They would not be laid to rest. While she felt proud of her work to clear their spirits as quickly as possible, it was hard to recover from everything she saw and experienced herself. She knew that the sheer magnitude of the event had cost Batya her own spirit. Why then, Gerti wondered, had she survived and been strong enough to continue with the work alone? What was the difference between her and the other spirits? Was this the only reason she had been created? For this one mission?

All of these questions did not prevent her from feeling sadness, a deep ache that lived within her. She loved each child spirit she had helped to escape; she adored Batya; and she missed her Hungarian family terribly. How could such a thing happen? How could she even have been asked to do such work? Did she have anything left to give if there was more planned for her?

She became overwhelmed by her thoughts and emotions. Why was she so alone? Where was Theo and why was he not showing her a path forward? Why should she stay in the grove? Her conclusion was that she should leave just as the others had. Only they had a destination and, even if they weren't aware of it, Gerti always knew where they were going. She wasn't so sure that she was meant for the same place or if she would ever reunite with the others. But she was ready to find out.

She headed to the portal of light where she had helped thousands of children and their families transition to the World to Come. The light was dimmer now, barely visible. She prepared to send herself off, breathing in one long and final goodbye. When it was time for her to enter the portal, she was unable to move forward. It was as if there was a wall that she could not penetrate. No matter how hard she tried, the portal would not receive her.

She returned to the grove and stood in the area where she and Batya had assisted the old village lady in ascending after finally overcoming her crippling guilt and anguish. But the spirit child was unable to connect to the energy needed to lift herself out. She moved to the very spot where Theo held Batya in his arms and transported her in a powerful whirlwind, a graceful ascension that matched Batya's spiritual beauty. But still she could not create the force needed for her own exit. Exhausted and desolate, she returned to the arms of the Mother Tree.

p n e u m a

CHAPTER TWENTY-NINE

Patti's new life continued to move at a slow pace down a meandering spiritual path. Shame, secrecy and extreme emotional danger no longer filled her days and nights. Now it was more about finding a balance between the comfortable, safe, clean life she had risked everything to achieve and her inner, spiritual life.

Knowing how much her sister was still struggling with the devastating impact of sexual abuse at the hands of their father, Patti wanted to find a way to tell their story, in her honor, because by now she knew that Kathy would never find her way out. And she never did.

Because Patti had letters, diaries, photographs, and other documentation of her amazing journey, she decided to write a book. It was very therapeutic to work on it now that she was able to revisit every aspect of her life without fear of emotional relapse. In fact, she felt like telling the story would be the centerpiece of her profound healing journey. Patti had always been a natural storyteller. The writing process would test her belief in being completely healed as she delved deeply into all the details that led to her reclaiming herself by building a tumor filled with her toxic past, having it removed, and rebirthing herself in a sterile room. Mostly she learned the power of telling the story. It came naturally to her, a grander version of the many monologues she had created that helped save her life.

Time passed in a very different way, less linear and more flowing. Learning to take things as they come, she became more open to

experiences that could not be planned or controlled. She was waiting, with no idea what for.

CHAPTER THIRTY

THEO FOUND GERTI perched on the sunny end of a long, thin branch of the grove's Mother Tree. She looked very young and small and fragile, but still vital. He alerted her to his presence and she turned her head, as if to tune in. And then he was there, next to her, his being so light it left no impression on the branch. Gerti was overjoyed to see him but didn't want him to recognize that right away because she was a little annoyed at how long he had left her there alone. He, of course, knew that and was happy to allow her need to assert herself in this way.

"Why am I the only one left here in the grove? All the other spirits have departed" she asked. Theo paused before answering. "What do you know about spirits, Gerti?"

"I know they are humans until death, then become spirits prior to departing for their final destination. And some stay longer than others. Like you."

Theo continued, "Do you believe that during the time you spent with your family in Hungary that you were a human?"

Gerti thought of her answer for a moment., "Maybe I wished I was, but I knew something about me was different. I didn't understand."

"You were not meant to understand until it was time. You knew enough to help those around you and you knew that they needed your help. That you didn't know why wasn't important. And you knew there were others like you somewhere because Batya came to be with you when Sandor died and you wanted to save him. You understood somehow that you must follow Batya's direction without being told why. And you knew you were like Batya and not the others, yes?"

Gerti nodded her head, beginning to arrange the pieces that Theo was laying out for her. "And I knew I was connecting Sandor's mother with his spirit at his funeral and that she felt his presence. I remember I told her that the dirt thrown on his casket was how the seedling that was his soul would be nurtured so he could always be with her."

"Yes, Gerti. You, too, are a seedling soul. The Spirit Council came together and created you from a small piece of Batya which we transported to your human mother's womb. You grew there until you were born so you could be with that community prior to the events which would lead them to the camp: partly so you could help them find their way through it, and partly because that human experience would best prepare you for what was to come. The level of suffering, the inhumanity, the pain needed to be understood at a soul level. Your work with the spirits came from that place. It is what made you different from the others. You were already a spirit when you were living in the human world. That is very rare. When did you first understand your power?"

"In the cattle car on the way to the camp. I didn't feel the physical suffering the way the others did. But I knew I could alleviate at least some of theirs and I naturally understood how. I helped the older couple transition together so they wouldn't be so afraid or feel alone. And I knew how to make Wally feel that she was taking care of me. That gave her purpose."

"Exactly,", said Theo, watching the story come to life within her. "Batya gave everything she had, all of her power, to getting the children, and then the families, out of the camp. She knew she could survive if she had been willing to stop after the last child left. But she couldn't do that. I knew staying for the other family members would end her spirit existence, but she was willing and wanted to make that sacrifice. I also knew that it would not be the end for you; it would make you stronger."

"So now it is time for me to go? And where will I go?" asked Gerti.

"No, it is not quite time. You will need help from a human to leave here."

"Why?" asked Gerti, showing disappointment and frustration that he was not offering an immediate path out of the grove for her as she had hoped.

"There is a human named Patti who has worked very hard to be ready and willing to help us. She is already a part of the spirit world even though she isn't dead; but she almost died while preparing. And she knows us. If you reach out to her, she will understand what happened here, what you did here. And she will tell the story. Part of the spirit mission we all care so much about must include telling the story. You will lead us in this final part of the work by introducing yourself to Patti and inviting her here to help you depart. It is time for the two of you to meet."

Theo opened his arms to Gerti and she climbed onto his lap and curled into him. "Will you stay with me a little longer?" she asked. "Yes," Theo said, "I will."

p n e u m a

CHAPTER THIRTY-ONE

ON A BEAUTIFUL SUNNY fall afternoon, Patti stepped outside to check the mail. As she headed to the gate that led to the street, she came to a stop, closed her eyes, turned her head to the side, and listened. It wasn't a voice, more like a message delivered straight to the knowing place, words not needed. It reminded her of a near death experience she had read about where a woman, as she was dying, knew precisely what to do and how to do it without being told. In Patti's case, the message was clear and concise. She was to go to Auschwitz.

It was surprising, this guidance, because Patti was not Jewish, had no family connection to the Holocaust or the war, and did not even know in which country the notorious Auschwitz was located. As she usually did in similar situations, although admittedly most of her other experiences did not involve traveling 5,942 miles to adhere to the guidance, Patti decided to wait and see if the direction was persistent or fleeting. By the end of the following day, an even clearer guidance was given that she was to be at the camp on November 2nd. She began taking it very seriously.

She called her teacher to ask for advice. Her trusted mentor said it was true guidance and suggested she go, if she felt like it was right for her. Patti asked what if she went to the camp on that day and nothing happened? Her teacher explained that something would happen, whether or not Patti was consciously aware of it, and the entire event was a leap of faith. But she believed that Patti was needed for a purpose, and it was not essential that she completely understand what that may be. Now or ever. She reminded Patti that she was particularly called to tragically touched places and there was barely another place on earth as tragically touched as Auschwitz.

She first said it out loud to a stranger at a garden show. "I'm going to Poland," Patti said, just to see how it sounded. She was still trying to come to terms with accepting, and following, the guidance of a voice she couldn't hear. She announced soon after to her husband that she was planning a trip to Poland. He asked why, and she responded that she was called to Auschwitz. As usual, he accepted her declaration and asked if he should travel with her. She replied that it was something she needed to do on her own. She began writing.

Arrangements were contemplated for arrival in time to spend November second at Auschwitz. For what purpose was still something I was holding only in faith.

In addition to learning about Krakow where I was planning to stay, I immediately began an intense education about the Holocaust through books, documentaries, and personal accounts. It came to my attention that November 1st is a Polish holiday. All Saints Day is known for its custom of placing flowers, lanterns and candles on graves to honor the dead. But what took my breath away was that November 2nd, the day on which I had engaged a driver and private Auschwitz guide, was All Souls Day, known as the Day of the Dead. A religious holiday in Poland, it is the day the living help the dead find their way to everlasting light. It is customary for the Polish people to leave their windows open that night to help the spirits escape and avoid being trapped on earth.

Nikki, my wonderful massage therapist, referred me to an acupuncturist as part of my preparation to travel. Rachelle was interested in my journey, in particular because her mother was a French Jew who worked for the resistance movement in France during World War II. She showed me a beautiful handmade document presented to her mother as a symbol of gratitude for her efforts to save Jews during the war. Also displayed on the wall of her studio was a beautiful old black and white photograph of she and her mother. Distinctive because it was shot in profile, mother and daughter facing each other with arms intertwined, she quietly said she believed that it reflected the love they shared. I was drawn to the photograph and would sometimes return to gaze at it while waiting to be called to the treatment room before departing.

Due to my large birthmark and the loss of forty lymph nodes prior to my bone marrow transplant, I had lived with numbness and a lack of feeling in my right upper arm for a long time. My oncologist did not want her to needle that arm, but she felt she could improve its circulation without directly treating it. During my first treatment, I could feel a rush of energy throughout the channels of my body. This was the most activity I had felt inside since making all my cells from scratch in my sterile room. The numbness subsided and I no longer felt blocked. For the first time since my illness, my body felt whole again. The acupuncturist told me to pay special attention when I arrived on the grounds of Auschwitz because she believed these treatment responses were related to my work there. It seemed that she and I had connected for a reason, but like every other part of the experience so far, the many questions did not yet have answers.

CHAPTER THIRTY-TWO

ONE OF THE LAST THINGS Patti did prior to her departure was to have a massage with Nikki. They had shared that amazing moment during the lowest point of Patti's bone marrow transplant when the dragonflies appeared in her room. She wanted to spend time with her before taking off on this mysterious journey. After a friendly chat, Nikki dimmed the lights and left the room so Patti could undress and prepare for the massage. She climbed onto the warm table and waited for Nikki to return.

Theo appeared holding Gerti's hand and their strong presence filled all the space in the room. She was feeling shy about showing herself to Patti and the other human, but she immediately knew that it was a safe place. Theo leaned in close to encourage her and said that she would determine the exact moment for the connection. He also noted that she may choose a different approach to each human, keeping in mind that Nikki's role was to encourage Patti to believe in the work she was being asked to do, not only here in this room, but also in the environment Patti would encounter at the camp.

Nikki stepped quietly into the room, lowered the lights further, and put on Michael Hoppe's album, *Solace*, the same music Patti always requested. As she relaxed into this final level of preparation for whatever awaited her, the touch and gentle movement of Nikki's hands took her to a meditative state. Gerti, choosing to appear in the clothing she was wearing when she arrived at the camp with her family, gently revealed herself to Patti who was deeply receptive to her presence. This first connection seemed familiar to both the human and the small spirit, even comfortable.

As Nikki worked on Patti's neck and upper chest, she was flooded with a vision of a young blonde girl walking across a large open field. Gerti chose that image because it was the walk from the train to the grove across the wind-blown field that became her transition from a partly human life experience to full-fledged spirit work. Nikki, too, was receptive to her appearance, and Gerti was pleased that she had accomplished the goal set out for her.

Theo beamed at his protégé in advance of their silent departure.

The massage ended, and Nikki left the room so Patti could get dressed. She paused before getting off the table, sensing the residue of the child's visit. She wanted to resist getting dressed so as not to break the spell, but knew it was late and she was the last appointment of the evening. When Nikki returned, they embraced with best hopes for the upcoming trip. As Patti put her hand on the exit door, Nikki rushed up behind her and said, "But what about the child?"

Patti turned her head in disbelief, asking, "Did you see the child?" Nikki nodded yes, she had seen a young girl during the session. They shared details of what they witnessed. Patti described the child as small and blonde with a white ribbon in her hair. Nikki gave the same physical description but saw her walking across a big, open field. There wasn't much more to say, each understanding that something related to Patti's mission had just happened to both of them at the same time. Nikki embraced Patti one last time and said she believed that her spirit was already there, in Poland, waiting for her body to arrive.

CHAPTER THIRTY-THREE

Armed with a deep and unknown sense of purpose, I began my journey. Once in Krakow, I arrived at my hotel on the beautiful Main Square and was escorted to my room. Over my bed was a painting of a young girl, older than the one in my vision, but of the same spirit. Her blonde hair was in pigtails with long, white ribbons. It was if she produced a magnetic field that constantly drew me to her, even in sleep.

On November 1ˢᵗ, in the late afternoon, the hotel called a cab to take me to the Rakowicki Cemetery for the All Saints Day celebration. While waiting on the corner of the Square, I saw a child bundled up against the evening chill watched over by her grandmother. She was younger than my spirit child, but possessed the same magnetic field as the painting upstairs in my room. I couldn't take my eyes off her as she twirled and played in the Square. I pointed at my camera and asked her grandmother if I could take a photograph. She smiled, obviously pleased, and agreed enthusiastically. Trying to collect the child for her photograph, she called her by name, my name. I snapped the photo, close up, and was astounded at the resemblance between myself at that age and the child, Patrycja in Polish, who shared my name.

The cab arrived to take me to the cemetery. What a sight to see all the graves ablaze with light from candles surrounded by flowers and religious symbols. As night fell, the haunting light from the thousands of candles reflected on the trees wearing their own blazing colors. All Saints Day in Poland is to celebrate saints, but also to remember friends and family members who have passed away. It was a beautiful combination of somber remembrance and joyful celebration of life.

The next morning, a car arrived at 8:30 a.m. to take me to Auschwitz. We traveled for about an hour along two lane roads through small villages in the pastoral Polish countryside. The driver pulled into the ordinary Auschwitz parking lot and accompanied me into the main building where he had obvious difficulty convincing the administrator that I had a reservation for a private guide that day. I couldn't understand the language but it was clear that she did not see my name on the list. He urged her to have another look and this time she located my name and sent us to the payment window with a smile. That is when Agnes suddenly appeared at my right side and all the tension left my body. I knew that I belonged in her hands for this day that had been on my mind for such a long while. She was clearly more than my Auschwitz guide.

We began our tour on that cold, grey windy morning under the famous arched sign ironically declaring "Arbeit Macht Frei," translated as "work sets you free." Agnes was in her mid-thirties, small in stature with short dark hair and no make-up. As we walked between the long red brick buildings of the camp, she explained that she was raised in Oswiecim, the small town where the camp is located, and began attending survivor meetings when she was fourteen-years-old. She was deeply moved by their stories and felt a calling to become a guide. It was obvious that she considered herself a guardian of this unthinkable history and a strong personal advocate for the poor souls who were brought to Auschwitz. It seemed vitally important to her in a nearly urgent way that I understand what these people endured on a daily basis. No detail was too small in order to make her case for the inhumanity of what happened on the very ground we were walking.

Agnes explained that people are often surprised to find that the Auschwitz portion of the camp has no railroad tracks or loading ramp. The trains arrived outside the gates and the prisoners were then herded to the camp on foot. There are tight rows of red brick buildings still surrounded by high barbed wire fences and guard towers. The gas chamber and crematorium are unexpectedly small, partially underground, and the entire camp has an almost claustrophobic feeling as one considers the huge numbers of people that were housed there. Around lunchtime, Agnes suggested we take a short break in the main building after which my driver would transport us to Birkenau, the larger more visually famous part of the camp.

After we parted, I reflected on the gravity of what I had witnessed at the notorious Auschwitz camp that morning. It was moving beyond description in the sheer weight of being present where such atrocities occurred. And yet, I had no clue as to why it was important for me to be there on that particular day.

Agnes woke my driver, who seemed to have been enjoying his easy day of waiting and napping in the Auschwitz parking lot, and the three of us headed out onto a two-lane rural road. She spoke quickly and firmly to him in Polish, gesturing and pointing. As we approached the main gate of Birkenau on the left side of the car—easily recognizable for its iconic red brick arched structure over the railroad tracks—she pointed for him to continue along the road. I could then see the perfectly symmetrical rows of barracks passing by, some brick, some wood, and some only a remaining foundation with a chimney. She explained that we were going to start at the back of the camp and make our way forward. She asked the driver to drop us on the side of the road and we took off on foot. She pushed open a heavy, tall chain link gate and closed it behind us. The brisk autumn wind howled through the huge open field that is Birkenau, approximately four hundred acres of beautiful green land, wide open compared to the cramped spaces of Auschwitz. It seemed like we were the only two people on earth at that moment.

We walked about halfway across the field and then turned deeper into the back of the camp on a soft, dirt path that led to a stand of mature trees of fading autumn colors. The trees were spaced well apart with thin, light trunks and high canopies. As is the case throughout both camps, authentic SS photographs documenting their unthinkable tasks, have been matched to the exact places where they were taken. Blown up and mounted, these heartbreaking images give the visitor a sense of exactly what occurred in that particular spot. As we approached the woods, Agnes pointed out the small man-made lake just off the path, one of several built by the Nazis to absorb never ending ashes from the busy crematoriums; a testament to the practical problems associated with death in such massive numbers. Tombstones in four different languages sit in front of the small lake honoring it as a grave site.

As I turned to face the stand of trees ahead, a large black and white photograph of mostly women and children casually waiting, resting in the very same trees, stared back at me. I was immediately drawn to one small child standing in a light-colored overcoat with dark collar, wool leggings and worn-out high-top boots with a ribbon in her short blonde hair. Her hands are cupped together and outstretched as if offering a gift. Instantly, I knew that this was the girl I had seen in my vision. She was the reason I was standing there in the woods of Birkenau on All Souls Day, the living being asked to help the dead. I was overcome by the enormity of this realization.

Agnes continued her dialogue by saying that these people would have just recently arrived on the train transport after days of traveling like cattle, having been instantly "selected" to die because they were mostly mothers and children, of no value to the Germans. They would have been walked through the open field to these woods, believing what they had been repeatedly told that this was to be their new home after having been relocated from their hometowns in Hungary. It is clear from the photograph that they had no idea that what they were waiting for was their turn in the very busy schedule of the gas chamber and crematorium complex just a short walk down the path to the clearing ahead. Agnes and I continued down the path just as they would have, just as that little girl did on the day the photograph was taken.

The gas chamber, undressing room, and crematorium structure is in ruins, exactly as it was left by the Nazis after they attempted to quickly destroy evidence of their crimes by blowing up the red brick *building prior to liberation. As we stood within the foundation of the building, Agnes showed me with sweeping gestures how odd and unusual it was for the Germans to put the undressing room between the gas chamber and the crematorium. This required the bodies to be hauled through the undressing room on their way to be burned so that those who believed they were about to have a nice shower could see the truth about what they were really facing. That was hard to think about, imagining the mothers suddenly realizing that they and their children were just moments from death. I took photographs while Agnes leaned against the partially destroyed brick wall, her head bowed as though in silent prayer.*

She slowly headed away toward a walking bridge but I couldn't follow any further. The need, the absolute requirement, for me to return to where the child was waiting overwhelmed me; and I explained to Agnes that I must go back to the woods. She said not to worry, that there were more woods up ahead. When I explained that it must be the woods we had already visited, she seemed confused, but reluctantly agreed to accompany me. Suddenly, Agnes stopped and asked if I would prefer privacy. With obvious relief, I accepted her sensitive offer and headed straight back down the path on my own.

Stepping into the grove, it was natural and easy to completely let go and surrender to what was happening, the inevitable event to which I had been called. No decision making was required, no thinking; just feeling and allowing. My body was trembling with emotion. The child's spirit was now fully present in the breeze, beneath my feet, between the branches, and in the falling leaves. I felt her gratitude as she led me through the steps to assure that after spending sixty-nine November seconds in this place of death, she would finally find her way to everlasting light on this All Souls Day.

I stepped into my place, intuitively knowing exactly where that was, and knowing with equal certainty if I veered away from it. Once there, I planted my feet a short distance apart with arms down by my side, raised my chin slightly, closed my eyes and breathed in the heavenly wind that was rolling across my face. Behind me, in the center of the stand of trees, I felt an energy gather and whip up, like a desert whirlwind, like a child's top spinning at its highest speed before it begins to wind down. Knowing not to look back, a stream of energy traversed every channel of my body, rooting me to the ground, and whistling through me with intention and a gentle ferocity. Never have I felt more connected to the earth, to another soul, or to myself. It lasted for a short while and then gradually diminished until my body was quiet, inside and out, and until the woods were still. At that moment, I felt a remarkably deep sense of peace. I turned around and stepped into the spot she had just inhabited and looked up to see the wide opening in the tree canopy that led to the endless grey sky. It was as if she had been launched by a cosmic rocket, creating the opening on her way out, on her way up. And she was gone, no longer present there with me. Assuming it would be difficult to ever leave this place, I was surprised to quickly come to the realization that there was now no reason to stay.

With my purpose understood for the first time, I walked back to the footbridge where Agnes waited patiently for me. Seeing her kind face and knowing she somehow understood, I burst into tears and she opened her arms to me, asking no questions. There was not another living soul around us.

We made our way to a long narrow building where prisoners who were selected for work were registered shortly after their arrival. It was very quiet as we walked alone through the haunting facility on a strange, raised glass tile floor. In the very back, there were large black boards displaying hundreds of photographs of Jewish families that had been found in the luggage of the final transports immediately prior to liberation. They included photos of weddings, babies, engagements, playing children, rabbis, and family gatherings. They offered a glimpse into the ordinary lives of those who were hauled away from their homes to camps like Auschwitz/Birkenau. It would have been easy to stay for hours looking into their lives, lingering on each face, every image. I stopped cold in front of one particular photograph of a mother and daughter, shot in profile, arms intertwined. It was strikingly similar to the one my acupuncturist kept in her studio of she her and her mother that had so attracted me as I prepared for my journey.

Agnes guided me through the remainder of the camp as the afternoon waned. As we prepared to part, I didn't know how to express my gratitude for what she had done for me on that November 2nd, for knowing exactly where I belonged and getting me there, and for her understanding, intuition and uncompromising compassion. We asked someone to take a photo before we said goodbye. I will never forget her.

When I returned to my hotel room that evening, the painting over the bed was just a painting, no longer drawing me in. Whatever energy had been alive in the image of the young girl with the white ribbons in her hair was no longer.

The rest of the trip was joyful and peaceful. Upon returning home, I told my husband, who had encouraged me to go to Poland alone to do whatever work awaited me there, the story of my afternoon at Birkenau. He said it was why I went.

I told my story to Nikki, who had shared my vision of the child and had described seeing her in an open field. She was deeply moved, especially hearing that the child had walked through a huge field on the day she arrived at Birkenau, the last day of her life. She also recognized her, as did I, from the photograph I showed her that guards the entrance to the woods.

I visited my acupuncturist who had helped me physically prepare for the experience by restoring circulation to my right arm so that energy could flow freely through my entire body, a requirement in order to accomplish the task I had been asked to do. I brought her a print of the photograph of the Jewish mother and child I had discovered just a short while after my experience in the woods that had so reminded me of the one of her and her mother. She was overcome when she saw it, moved to tears, and said that it looked familiar to her. She said that it was mostly children that her mother saved during the war.

I took my photographs and stories with me to visit my teacher in

Sedona. She was very proud of my willingness to follow the calling that sent me to Poland and understood that I was needed to help the spirit of a child be released from the camp. I explained to her how angry I was to think of that child's spirit being left in that terrible place for so many long winters. She explained that it would be like an instant to a spirit and that, for whatever reason, she was waiting for me to join her there before she could depart.

CHAPTER THIRTY-FOUR

For several years after her visit to the camp, Patti lived a happy, quiet life always staying open to her spirit work.

She felt tremendous gratitude for the opportunity she had been given in Poland; but, while she believed she had done what was asked of her, she couldn't overcome the feeling that there was more work to do. Like a mission that had not yet been completed. Haunted by the feeling, she had no guidance as to what more she could offer. She also knew that seeking spiritual answers could often be a lengthy process that required patience and faith. So she waited.

pneuma

CHAPTER THIRTY-FIVE

Once Gerti ascended from the grove, where her spirit life began in earnest, she arrived at her next phase of existence. It was unclear where she was but she knew certain things. It was not earth where she had lived with a human family her first four years and accompanied them to the "little meadow of birches," the Birkenau camp. None of the thousands of spirits she had helped usher out of the camp were present at her current location.

But from her new vantage point, she had extraordinary vision. She could "see" things happening in different places and times but had no idea why this ability had been assigned to her. She had learned from her experience in the grove after the others left that sometimes she was to simply exist in her environment until guidance appeared. So she settled into her new home and waited.

It gradually became clear to her that not only could she see these things happening in other places, she could actually transport herself to those places to witness the various happenings. In this way, she could begin to understand what her purpose may be in those situations. She knew that Theo was not only her superior and beloved mentor, but he also was spirit guide to many others, including humans. One of those others was Patti, who had been under Theo's watchful eye since she was born. Theo had known for a very long time of the connection between Gerti and Patti and how they would eventually meet, launching each of them to their new phase.

As part of her vision, Gerti could see Patti and how her life had unfolded since being called to the camp. Patti still felt uncertain as to what her new phase would be, just as Gerti gradually tried to understand her own. They both made the assumption that it was independent work and, maybe at some future time, they would be reunited.

CHAPTER THIRTY-SIX

PATTI WAS NOW FEELING a stronger sense of urgency to understand the purpose that would make her experience at the camp feel resolved. To that end, she signed up for one of her teacher's courses, thinking it would help her connect to this unknown purpose. One evening the subject of the class was how to make contact with your spirit guides. On that night, for the first time, Patti saw Theo clearly, in a tree. There were other spirits present, but she could only see him. He felt instantly familiar, and she knew that, while she was "seeing" him for the first time, it was a presence that had been with her since her earliest years, particularly during pivotal moments that shaped the direction of her life. Soon after, she gradually, but with great certainty, grew into the knowledge that she was to tell the story of her experience in the grove, not just what happened to her, but what happened there over fifty-six days in the spring of 1944.

She wanted to tell the story of Batya, the beautiful and elegant ballerina spirit, who was assigned the mission of guarding the souls of the Hungarian Jews, particularly the children, before and after they were brutally murdered in the gas chamber. She wanted to tell how Batya begat the seedling soul of Gerti, and how, with the help of the other spirits, she transported the seed to the womb of a Hungarian Jewess who would birth her and give her the only human experience she would ever have including a beloved grandmother, father, and sister. She wanted to tell of Gerti's first three years of love and friendship with her family as she gradually grew into her spirit powers. She wanted to tell of the compassion and sweetness, love and joy that emanated from this young spirit child, even when the darkness was so close. She wanted to tell the story of Batya and Gerti, the two spirits who together threw sparkle and stars down the path of death and lifted the thousands of brand-new little spirits straight to the portal of light that would lead them out of the camp to the World to Come. She wanted to tell what a comfort they were to the children so they wouldn't be scared or trapped in the misery of their last human circumstance. She wanted to tell how she wordlessly heard the guidance to travel to the camp and how Gerti dramatically appeared to her and her close friend to introduce herself so Patti would recognize her when she arrived at the camp and saw her iconic photo, her sweet smile, with arms extended and hands cupped toward the Nazi photographer. And she wanted to describe the opportunity to fully experience Gerti's presence in the grove and to be a witness to her glorious ascension, just as Gerti had witnessed Batya's in Theo's arms, completely spent from the hard work of overseeing the transition of over 400,000 spirits. And she wanted to honor Theo, who had been a constant presence in her own life, saving her only when she wasn't strong enough to save herself. The strongest bond between Gerti and Patti was Theo, his vision of their potential and the work of which they were capable, together.

But she wasn't ready to know these things quite yet. That would require Gerti's help.

CHAPTER THIRTY-SEVEN

After watching Gerti discover her new powers on her own, Theo knew it was time for a visit. He was constantly amazed at how patient the little spirit could be even when she felt forgotten or lonely. But she could be just as feisty as Patti was when she asked God to remove her birthmark, and just as angry when God didn't go along.

Gerti found herself in a blank, white space rarely inhabited by other spirits. The highest level of workers made this their home, but their work was out in the world so they rarely spent time there. Decision-making took place in the whiteness, missions were identified and committed to, and assignments were made. Theo was the decision maker in all things and was extraordinarily active as the missions were implemented—very different from his predecessor who rarely left the whiteness. Now he was feeling tired, despite being energized by the glorious abilities of the small spirit who had outperformed his most ambitious expectations. On her own, she had already made her way to areas of interest and was thinking in terms of who needed help and in what form. It was time to assign her a mission that would bring the Birkenau mission full circle, and bring her and Patti together in that sacred resolution.

Theo knew that Patti would struggle to find a way to tell the entire story, beyond what she had actually witnessed. He knew that she would understand her own experience over time, and that she would research the historical significance of those fifty-six days in the spring of 1944. But how would she be able to tell Gerti's story, and that of the hundreds of thousands of Jews who perished in Birkenau over such a short period of time? How would she know what life was like for them prior to being herded to the camp? Because they were very real people, she wanted to appropriately honor them and their horrific sacrifice and unbearable loss. He knew that, with Gerti's help, she could sense their stories but she would need encouragement and validation.

Patti had made efforts to be in contact with Gerti again after their time together in the grove but had received nothing back. It took a while for her to realize that the ability to tell the story was coming from Gerti, not from her own hand. The guidance was clear and true and, remarkably, had a deep sense of familiarity to it, as though Patti had been a part of it all along. Only Theo knew for sure how interconnected they were, and for how long. Patti and Gerti finished the mission together with conscious intention.

When Theo approached Gerti to discuss this final phase of the work, she understood and was already connecting to Patti to help fill in the spaces of her blank page, her version of Gerti's white space. Gerti no longer needed Theo's constant presence. Nor did Patti. He would always be there for them, but, understanding their growing independence, he was able to contemplate what the end of this highly important mission meant for him. It would be his last. But he had one final duty as head of the Spirit Council: he would rename his successor to symbolize that she had completed her mission as Gerti and was now taking her place in the world of spirt, soul, breath, and air. She would be known as "pneuma."

On a beautiful sunny fall afternoon, similar to the day that Patti first heard the guidance to go to Auschwitz many years before, she gazed out the huge bay window of her writing room to the mother maple tree that stood watch over her brood of six others, their leaves floating to the ground in the breeze that caused the Corinthian chimes to call out in their haunting way. Her storytelling was finished, and she contemplated how the narrative would find its way into the world.

pneuma

pneuma

CHAPTER THIRTY-EIGHT

The sprawling oak tree in the open field came to life at twilight, buzzing with dragonflies, ladybugs, bees, birds and fireflies creating color, sound, movement and light. The spirits were lingering and visiting and looking forward to their first meeting under new leadership. Pneuma's appearance on the tree's highest branch was illuminated by her bright white spirit light. As she called the meeting of the Spirit Council to order with a gentle wave of her hand, the others emerged throughout the tree to take part. Their shared energy caused a vibration throughout the old oak that resonated with each spirit attendee and penetrated to every distant root in the open field. Pneuma opened her arms to them and said, "Welcome all! We have much work to do." In response, the collective light of the spirits flooded the tree.

Theo watched from the whiteness.